SILLY RABBITS

THE POPE LICK MASSACRE 2

ERIC BUTLER

Naked Cat Press

Silly Rabbits: The Pope Lick Massacre 2
Copyright © 2023 by Eric Butler.

This book is a work of fiction. Names, characters, businesses, organizations, places, events, and incidents either are the product of the author's imagination or are used fictitiously. Any resemblance to actual persons, living or dead, events, or locales is entirely coincidental.

For information contact:

Naked Cat Press
http://www.nakedcatpress.com
nakedcatpress@gmail.com

Book design by Naked Cat Press
Edited by Lisa Lee Tone
Cover design by Naked Cat Press

ISBN: 978-1-7341795-9-0

First Edition: Oct 2023

10 9 8 7 6 5 4 3 2 1

PRAISE FOR SILLY RABBITS

"Eric Butler captures the spirit of Pope Lick in a beautifully terrifying way. A much-anticipated sequel that lives up to its predecessor. Beware of Pope Lick, be AWARE of Eric Butler." – Stuart Bray, Author of *Broken pieces of June*.

"The Goat Man is fucking creepy. Turn your lights on and tuck your feet under the covers, this one's gonna getcha." - Rayne Havok, Author of *Necrosis*

"Eric Butler brings us back to the woods of Pope Lick for the much-anticipated continuation of the bloodshed. Half Man. Half Goat. All sequel. All hail the Goatman." – M Ennenbach, Author of *Cuckoo*

"In this sequel to Pope Lick Massacre, Butler kicks murder and mayhem into high-gear. Character driven and action packed, the blood flows like water straight through to the last page. You've never read Butler like this before." - Candace Nola, author of *Bishop*.

"I grew up in the area, and we used to taunt the Goatman, wishing he'd come out and mimic our voices. If I had read this book 25(+) years ago, I would have never taken the chance and left the Goatman alone." – Sea Caummisar, Author of the *Raised by a Killer* series

"PLM2 continues the Goatman's thrilling bloodfest and delivers on both emotional terror and splatter-fueled mayhem. Highly recommend." - D.W. Hitz, author of *Stay Out of the Tub*

"In small town USA, it ain't uncommon to see someone leading a goat to slaughter. But here in Pope Lick ... it's the other way around. Butler brings it again in this brutal follow-up to the original. Read this... if you dare!" - Merrill David, Author of *Season Pass*

TO ALL THE SILLY
RABBITS OUT THERE.
THANK YOU FOR
READING.

INTERLUDE ONE

"Hello? Is anyone there? Please, for the love of God ... I'm scared of the dark ... please."

CHAPTER ONE

Billy Doogan leaned against his pickup truck. He parked on the edge of the Parkland's Soccer Complex lot, kept back by the yellow police tape. He figured any closer and he might grab the attention of the two deputies standing on the other side. He had a man on the inside anyway. Dipshit better deliver. He sighed, well aware that, at best, it was going to be fifty-fifty.

His phone vibrated. He slipped it from his pocket and stared at the caller ID for a moment before answering. "What's up, Simon?"

"Is it true?"

"Not sure," Billy replied. "They have the whole area taped off and a couple of Barney Fifes on duty. I can't get any closer without causing a scene. Hopefully, your boy Tristan comes through."

"He called you, didn't he?" Simon asked with a huff. "You want a criminal empire, it's gonna require people like Tristan. Trust me."

"You have to earn that, buddy boy," Billy said, spitting off to the side. "How's the rest coming along?"

"Pete thinks a day or so and we'll be up and running. Jay also said there's a shitload of weed growing out there."

Billy offered a grunt into the phone. *Finally, a silver lining.* "Things are starting to look up for us ...," he trailed off, his attention on the row of paramedics carrying covered stretchers toward the ambulances parked behind the yellow tape. "I'll call you back."

A woman holding a microphone turned to face the cameraman. Her expression grew serious while the man counted down from three. *Here's my chance.* Billy pushed off his truck and moseyed in the opposite direction of the news crew. The deputies moved as one towards the newswoman as she began her spiel.

"As you can see, there is a steady stream of bodies coming from the woods behind us. The police have not issued a statement yet, but stay with WLKY for the latest developments on what this reporter can only call a massacre."

Billy glanced over, making sure she still held the deputies' attention. He slipped under the yellow tape and made a beeline for the ambulances. The paramedics arrived and laid the stretchers down on the sidewalk. Five of the men turned and began to walk back the way they came; the sixth moved over to the last blood-soaked sheet and pulled back the corner.

"I didn't know you were also a paramedic," Billy said, stepping over to the body.

Tristan shook his head. "Just helping. So is this the guy y'all were looking for?"

Billy squatted, lined up his phone, and snapped a picture. *Fucking Fitz.* "Yeah, he was the one bragging about taking over everything. Any idea what went down?"

"Something crazy. They're still finding parts all over the place."

Billy patted Tristan on the shoulder and stood. "Well, good work. Let me know if they find anyone else of interest."

He walked back to his truck. Fitz wasn't smart enough to be the brains behind any new operation. *Not in a million years.* But maybe if Billy's luck continued, whoever was in charge would now be dead somewhere out in those woods.

Simon dropped his phone on the table and glanced at the television. The cameraman zoomed in on a line of stretchers exiting the woods. *Jesus Christ ... what have I gotten myself into?* The doorbell rang, and for a moment, he contemplated ignoring it, but whoever was outside held the button down.

"Chill," he called out, stomping to the front door. He pressed his eye to the peephole and found two men standing on his porch. The first was a giant, standing at six feet five inches and weighing easily over three bills. The other man was his opposite in every way. With a sigh, he opened the door. "What are y'all assholes doing here?"

"Trying to make up for that mix-up last week," the giant said with a crooked smile. He held up a six-pack of Kentucky Ale. "We even brought your favorite."

Simon stepped back and motioned for them to enter. He reached down to grab a bottle as they passed and then closed the door. "I'm not the one y'all need to kiss up to, but I'll drink your beer, Mike."

"Lenny and me just want another shot. Figured if anyone could convince Billy, it would be his right-hand man."

Simon grunted and motioned for them to take a seat at the table. Between Mike's bulk and Lenny's tendency to skip showering, he wasn't about to let them sit on his sofa. The dining room chair groaned in protest when Mike sat. Lenny stood off to the side, staring blankly at the television.

"They just carried out a shitload of bodies from the woods over by Parkland," Simon said between sips. His phone issued a ding, and he reached over to unlock it. A picture popped up on the screen. "This the guy you two fuck-ups thought would be running things soon?"

Mike and Lenny glanced at Simon's phone and then at each other before Mike spoke. "Well, not him exactly. I said we're sorry."

Lenny offered a shrug and then turned his attention back to the television. Simon hadn't expected Lenny to say anything, the man hadn't spoken a word in the three years since he'd known him, but he also didn't expect such a laissez-faire attitude about it.

He gulped down the rest of his beer and motioned for another. "Just lay low, and I'll talk to Billy about it."

"Thanks," Mike said with a grin. He slid the beers closer and stood. "We won't let y'all down again."

CHAPTER TWO

Jay glanced up. He swore he could hear something echoing down the tunnels. He reached over and tapped Pete on the shoulder. "Do you hear that?"

Pete stopped drilling and pulled his headphones off his right ear. "What?"

"Thought I heard something," Jay said, standing and walking to the far entrance. "Like some kind of knocking."

"These old caves and tunnels are terrible with acoustics," Pete said with a shrug. "Probably just the noise we're making coming back at us."

"Yeah ... maybe. Let's get the last of the lights hung so we can get out of these tunnels."

"Give me a sec," Pete said, starting the drill back up.

Jay shined his flashlight down the tunnel, sweeping it back and forth. *Nothing.* He stepped to the next opening and shined the light but again found nothing. His head tilted, and he strained to hear the noise again. The drill cut off, but there was only silence.

"Now all we have to do is attach these last few lights, connect the pipes to the turbines, and Bob's your uncle," Pete said with a grin, throwing his drill back into his bag. He hooked the wire to the wall and checked the plugs.

"So, you think this is actually going to work?"

"Sure do. I was doubtful when Simon said he thought there might be a power source in these caves, but he was right. System should run itself once I get it put together."

Thunk, schwipe, thunk.

"There." Jay spun in a circle, unsure where the noise was coming from. "Did you hear it that time?"

Pete scooped up his bag. "Probably an animal. Hopefully, not a bear."

"A bear?" Jay whispered, his eyes growing wide. The flashlight beam began to tremble.

"Jesus," Pete said with a chuckle, clicking on his light. "It's probably a wild pig or a goat. Come on, the sooner this gets done, the sooner we can get back out in the fresh air." He did a quick sweep of the chamber and started towards the closest tunnel.

Jay stood still for a moment, until Pete called out, "Let's go."

He shook his head and hurried to catch up. They had been underground for days, and although he felt fine at the beginning, he was now at his breaking point. His gaze fell on Pete's back, and he sighed. With the setup almost complete, Jay would have to finish the last part of the job. Billy had been very clear during their last phone call about what would happen if he didn't get it done.

Pete stopped periodically, checking the lines and plugs before continuing to the next grouping. Jay stood right behind him while he worked, swinging his light back and forth.

Thunk, schwipe, thunk.

"Fuck me," Jay said, his voice going up an octave.

They continued down the tunnel. A low roar began, growing in volume with each step they took. *At least I won't be able to hear whatever that noise is anymore.* He flashed his light behind them, relieved when the light fell only on

9

stone. Jay swallowed and pressed his hand to his chest, surprised his heart hadn't burst out like that alien from the movies.

They turned the final corner, and the roar became deafening. *Just up ahead.* He grinned nervously and fought the urge to laugh. Once started, he wasn't sure he'd be able to stop. He waited for Pete to disappear and then stepped to the fissure. They missed it the first couple of times, which meant walking the long way through the tunnels every time they needed to come back.

He wiggled into the opening, holding his breath to slip past the tight spot before stepping into a large chamber. Old junk filled most of the room. Simon told them to gather everything up and put it out of the way. Jay was still amazed at all the stuff they found abandoned down here. He hoped Billy would let them go through it once they were up and running. Who knew what hidden treasures they might find. His smile broadened at the thought.

Pete walked across the room, pausing to shine a light on three large wooden chests pressed against the wall. They had spent hours guessing what might be in there, but now, Jay simply wanted to be done.

"Well?" he hollered, trying to be heard over the water's roar.

Pete held up a finger. He turned his attention to the generators over in the far corner, checking the setup before plugging in the wiring they had just completed. With a thumbs up, he flicked a switch on each one. Jay's hand slipped into his back pocket, his fingers wrapping around the smooth wooden handle of his folding knife. Pete stood up and clicked off his light.

Jay followed suit, plunging them into darkness. He fought the urge to turn it back on. He knew it was impossible, but he swore he could hear those sounds once again.

Thunk, schwipe, thunk.

His attention darted to tiny flickers of light on the far wall. *Please work.* He removed the knife from his pocket, using his thumb to pop out the four-inch blade.

Pete let out a loud cry and jumped to his feet, his arm extended to receive a high five. Jay reached out, grabbed his wrist, and jerked Pete closer, causing him to stumble. The blade slipped into his belly, and Jay wrapped his free arm around the man's back. Pain quickly washed away the shock in Pete's eyes as Jay twisted the knife.

"What the fuck?"

Jay couldn't hear the question, but he saw Pete's lips form the words before his jaw went slack and the light faded from his eyes. *Nothing personal.* He didn't speak, surprised to find a lump in his throat. He dragged the body to the water and pushed it in, careful to avoid all of Pete's hard work. He dunked the knife into the icy water to wash the blade clean.

With a sigh, he stood. Billy's voice echoed in his head: *Make sure it works before you leave.* He had to grab his pack anyway. He glanced at the water one last time and stepped from the chamber. Lines of light offered a soft glow throughout the tunnels, and he smiled. *Holy shit. It works.*

Jay rushed down the tunnel, the water's roar growing softer until there was only the sound of his footsteps. He followed the arrows they painted with reflective paint, confident that they would lead him to their packs. *Guess I have dibs on Pete's stuff.*

He turned the corner and froze.

Thunk, schwipe, thunk.

Jay gripped his knife tighter.

Thunk, schwipe, thunk.

He stared at the opening in front of him, positive the noise was coming from their campsite. The startled cry of a goat came from the darkened doorway, and he let loose a sigh. *Pete was right ... thing's probably caught in one of the bags.*

Jay stepped through the opening and glanced around. *Stinky bastard.* The room was heavy with shadows, the light from the tunnels barely making it past the makeshift doorway. Biting his bottom lip, Jay suddenly feared he'd dispatched Pete too soon. He clicked on his flashlight.

A figure crouched across the room. It reached out and dragged one of their bags closer, dug through it, and threw it against the wall. *Thunk, schwipe, thunk.* It threw back its head and sniffed. Jay's bladder released, the hot urine soaking into his jeans. He clenched his ass, fearful his bowels were next, as his light illuminated the figure's head. *Are those horns?*

The creature stood, turning to face him. Jay wanted to run away but remained frozen while his eyes swept over the thing before him. It stood on black hooves, with coarse dark hair running up to its belly and a thick penis swaying limply between its legs. Dark smears of unrecognizable filth and gore decorated the creature's skin. The hair grew thick once more at its shoulders and covered its head. Jay shuddered when their gazes locked, the creature's square, unblinking eyes staring at him. *Oh my God.*

Its mouth cracked open into a broad grin. "What do we have here?" it asked in an oddly familiar voice.

The Goatman stepped closer, and the flashlight slipped from Jay's numb fingers. Flashes of light began to spark across the walls and soon bathed the room in a soft glow. His legs gave way, and he dropped to his knees.

The Goatman raised its arm high over its horns, the light reflecting on the head of the hatchet suddenly clutched tight in its fist. Its arm drove down, the blade slamming into Jay's forehead with a sickening crack.

Billy's not going to be happy about this.

He wanted to laugh at the absurdity of that thought, but all he could manage was a gurgle. His eyes rolled up, catching the creature's awful smile.

"Good night, little rabbit."

He swore it was Pete speaking, but that was impossible.

That's impossible. Pete's dead ... right?

CHAPTER THREE

A shadow fell over Simon. He opened his eyes, surprised to find his sister standing there. She held out a bottle of water, and after a moment, he took it.

"What are you doing here?" he asked, sitting up to take a long drink.

"Don't you remember?" she replied, holding up her backpack. "Mom's going out of town with the newest asshole."

He didn't but nodded and offered a sympathetic smile. "Well, you're always welcome here."

She dropped her pack and stretched out on the other lawn chair. "So, what's the plan?"

"Your brother already has plans," a harsh voice called out from the side of the house.

"Jesus," Simon said, standing. "Does anyone knock?"

"I did," April offered, "but you didn't answer."

He glanced at his sister, unwilling to explain that the reason he didn't answer was now standing before them. "Sup, Billy?" he asked, bumping fists, knowing the man wouldn't lower his hand until they did. "What brings you around?"

"I'm hoping you're gonna tell me you've heard from Jay."

"Why would he call me?" Simon replied. "You made it clear that you're in charge."

Billy's smile widened. "And yet no one does what they're told. I'm thinking we should head up and see if Jay's speakin' the truth."

Simon frowned and motioned to his sister. "Can't today."

"Ah, bullshit ... Honey, can you go inside and grab me and your brother a beer?"

April glanced between the two men and, after a slight nod from Simon, slid open the patio door and disappeared inside. Billy waited until the door clicked back in place before jabbing his finger into Simon's chest.

"Listen up, *partner*," he growled. "Time is running out for us to take over the market. If we don't seize this opportunity, some other motherfuckers will. We need to start cookin' and, if Jay's not full of shit, start harvesting all that weed he swears is out there. We can't afford to just sit here and wait."

"I'm not draggin' my baby sister—"

"Unless you're suddenly flushed with green, you ain't got much choice," Billy said, turning to face April as she stepped back outside. He took the beer and cracked it open. "How would you like to join us for a little hike?"

★★★

"Jesus Christ, Beth," Martin groaned. "If I'd have thought me getting fucked today just meant walking twenty-five miles, I might have passed."

She spun around; her left eyebrow raised as a wide smile bloomed on her face. She continued to walk backward, adding an exaggerated sway to her hips. He imagined pulling her t-shirt over her head to expose her breasts, his eyes following her tan lines to tiny triangles of pale skin. He licked his lips, moving his gaze to her hips, where he pictured his hands for a moment. He envisioned his hands sliding to the button of her cut-off jeans and then her wiggling out of the denim until her shorts lay on the path. His eyes glazed over, and he wanted nothing more than to fall to his knees and bury his face into her crotch. The sound of snapping fingers pulled him from his daydream.

"Who said anything about you getting to fuck me?" she asked, her voice thick with desire. "Maybe I lured you out here to kill you. Sacrifice you to some dark god."

"Well, that's fine as long as I at least get some head," he said, speeding up to close the space between them.

She laughed, her eyebrows waggling in mock excitement. The space between them closed quickly, and he reached out to grab her. She darted to the side, her laughter shifting to a shocked cry as he tumbled by and disappeared into the foliage.

"Oh shit. Shit. Shit," he cried out, each word punctuated by a grunt.

Beth stood frozen, hoping to hear him say something more but finding only silence. A tremor ran up her spine. *What are you doing?* She sprang forward, stepping over a thick root that arched through the path. She glanced down, noting the slope of the ground. Stepping from the path, she pressed into the woods. Beth began to lean back, taking each step carefully as the ground went from a gradual tilt to suddenly quite steep. "Martin!" she called out, praying he was all right. She shifted to the left, noting a worn trail leading down from the path.

"Martin! Hold on, I'm coming," she shouted.

Beth continued down, fighting the urge to rush ahead. She slid to a stop, pulling up just as her toes slipped over the edge of a drop-off. She leaned forward. Martin lay sprawled out below; his backpack dangled from a tree branch a few feet above his head. Her breath caught as she stared. *Oh, God ...*

He laid on his back, arms spread wide and his left leg twisted unnaturally, stuck off to the side. *He's so still.*

Martin's eyes shot open; a groan followed.

"Oh, thank God," Beth said with a relieved laugh. "I thought you were dead."

"Aren't I?" he said through gritted teeth. "Jesus, everything hurts." Taking a deep breath, he shifted. A cry of pain slipped past his lips, and he grew still. His breaths came quick, and he began to pant.

"What is it?"

"Think my leg is broken," he said through gritted teeth, pushing up to rest on his elbows. He studied his leg and, after a moment, sighed. "Yeah, that's not right. Fuck. I don't think I can stand, let alone walk."

"I'll carry you," she said, the words ringing hollow in her ears.

"And how are you going to get me out of here?" he asked, locking eyes with her. He tried to hide the pain but failed miserably. "It's at least a fifteen-foot drop ... hell, maybe twenty. You need to go find help."

Beth squatted at the edge, going over the situation in her mind. She sighed. *God damn it, he's right.* If she went down there, she couldn't see a way to get him back up. She gazed off into the distance, seeing only an endless wash of greens and browns. Without the path, she wasn't sure she could navigate them back to the car from down there.

"Seriously," he hissed. "I'm not sure how long I can take this, so will you please go and find help?"

"Yes, sorry," she said, trying to hold back tears. "I was just seeing if there might be a way out from down there."

Martin glanced around, leaning his head all the way back at the end. "There's nothing that suggests a path or any other way out of here. Just go get help, and y'all can lift me back up."

Beth stood, kissing her finger before reaching out to point it at him. He returned the gesture, a tortured smile on his lips.

"Okay … I'll be back. Just don't go anywhere," she said, moving back to the path.

"Fuck you," he called out with a grunted laugh.

Beth paused as she stepped back on the path to tie a handkerchief to the closest branch. She took a deep breath and started to jog back the way they came. With a little luck, she thought she could be back in an hour. Two at the most.

CHAPTER FOUR

"Are we lost?" Amber asked, her tone light and innocent.

Scott glanced over, finding her watching him with a sly smile. She batted her eyes before a bout of giggles slipped out. He offered a grunt and a roll of his eyes, then moved his attention back to the road. *Of course we're lost.* But it would be a cold day in hell before he admitted it out loud.

How was I to know our carrier had no service out here? He grimaced, ignoring the memory of Amber suggesting they should print out a hard copy. *Pretty sure I'll be hearing about this for quite a while.*

"Honey, I have to go to the bathroom," Amber said as a gas station sign appeared ahead.

He nodded, afraid of what might come out if he opened his mouth. The last thing he needed was to start a fight right off the bat. He turned into the lot and parked. She leaned over and planted a kiss on his cheek.

"Sweetie, quit being stubborn," she said, opening the door before slipping out of the car. "Go ask for directions."

He watched her walk inside, blowing out the breath he hadn't realized he was holding. *She's right.* Shaking his head, he got out. Amber reappeared with a large brick with a chain and key dangling from it. Her eyebrows rose, and she puckered her lips to blow him an exaggerated kiss. He couldn't help but smile; his eyes locked onto her ass as she disappeared around the corner in search of the restroom. A sudden urge to follow her overwhelmed him. His head cocked to the side as he thought about it. *There'll be plenty of time during the trip,* he finally decided, and instead moved to the door.

A bell announced Scott's entrance. The man behind the counter looked up from a magazine, his eyes enlarged from the thick lenses on his glasses. He offered a broad smile, exposing several missing teeth, then lifted his ballcap and ran his fingers through the greasiest hair Scott had ever seen before pulling it back down. Scott stopped a few feet from the counter, surprised to find the magazine was the latest *Playboy* open to the centerfold. *Jesus, I hope reading was all he was doing.*

"So, your lady friend says you're lost," the man said, his words slightly slurred together. Scott nodded, wondering if there was something more than soda in his cup. The man took a sip and pointed to the display stand by the register. "These here are maps. They help folks find their way."

He snickered, and Scott's cheeks grew hot. *Keep it cool*, he reminded himself, knowing how upset Amber got when he lost his temper. He forced a smile on his lips and pulled out one of the maps.

"Thanks ... good to know," he said, forcing his jaw to relax. "So we're trying to find the Parklands. I was sure it was off I-265."

The man nodded and lifted a different cup to his mouth. He spat out a glob of black goo and pointed with his free hand to a spot on the map. "This is us," he said before drawing his finger across the page. "And you want to go here, for some Godforsaken reason."

Scott looked up, surprised to find the man no longer smiling. "What do you mean?"

The man shook his head and frowned. "Didn' you hear? Some sicko hacked up a bunch of people out there. News lady said parts were *missing*. You'd be better off taking that little

lady of yours to the nearest motel and butterin' those biscuits."
He barked out a laugh and slapped his hand on the counter.

Scott forced an awkward smile to his lips. "That's funny; the brochure didn't mention that."

"No shit. I'm pretty sure they don' want people thinkin' some lunatic is out there killin' hikers. Or worse, the legend is true ..." He trailed off, staring past Scott.

What the fuck is he talking about? Scott followed the man's gaze and saw Amber outside, his question suddenly forgotten. He watched her, a smile growing on his lips. She stood by the car, resting her arm on the hood. She was just under six feet tall, with legs that seemed to go on forever, the illusion exaggerated by her love of cutoff shorts and ankle socks. Today, she wore her favorite Coors Light t-shirt, a light red with the logo in silver. It was his favorite too, ever since he accidentally shrank it in the wash. She complained that every movement made it ride up and expose her stomach, but he didn't mind.

It was her idea for them to spend a week out in the wilderness to rehab his knee. She promised to go easy on him, but he could barely keep up with her track and field training when he was one hundred percent. Still, anything was better than playing catch with the pitching coach. She offered a small wave when she noticed they were watching. Scott waved back and sighed. *How did I get so lucky?*

"I can think of three reasons she's with you, and after meetin' ya, I'm confident it's not looks or personality," the man said, disbelief plain on his face. Scott turned his attention back, smiled, and offered a shrug. The man rolled his eyes and pulled a pen from his shirt pocket and circled a spot on the map. "Y'all seem like a nice couple, so if you wanna camp or hike or whatever without the worrying about being murdered, this is the place."

"Okay, thanks. So, how much?" he asked as he gestured to the map.

The man folded it up and handed it to Scott with an exaggerated wink. "It's free, but you have to promise to have her call you Jimmy the next time you're givin' it to her." The man's coarse laughter followed Scott out the door.

"Jesus ... That was weird," Scott grumbled as he slid into the driver's seat.

Amber slipped her shoes off and threw them in the back seat. She reached over and placed her hand on his thigh. She gave an affectionate squeeze and smiled.

"Thanks," she purred, leaning closer.

She grabbed the map and turned his head so they were face to face. Her hand slid up his thigh, stopping to rest on his crotch. She kissed him, softly at first, but as she started to rub her hand up and down, her kiss became hungrier. He groaned, and her tongue entered his mouth. *I should ask for directions more often.* His hand slipped under her shirt and slid across her warm, soft skin.

He gently massaged her left breast, feeling her nipple harden. She moaned, her hand fumbling with his waistband. A loud knock made Amber squeak and pull away. Scott looked around in confusion and found the man from inside bent over, staring through the driver's side window and holding up the bathroom key.

"That's Jimmy with two Ms." He roared with laughter as Scott started the car and pulled away.

CHAPTER FIVE

"Man, I don't recognize anything," Simon said, glancing around and seeing nothing but nature in all directions.

"What the fuck?" Billy snapped, spinning around. "I thought you knew where it was."

Simon shrugged. "Sorta ... in relation to the hospital, but none of this looks familiar."

"Dammit, I put you in charge so one of us would know where to go."

"And I told you where we needed to start from to do that, but you wanted to find that special *grass* Jay said was out here first," Simon said, lowering his voice and glancing back to make sure his sister didn't overhear.

"I'm not gonna make it," April said between huffed breaths when she drew closer.

Simon frowned, stopping to let her catch up. Sweat poured down her face, dripping from her chin and hair as if she'd just stepped out of the shower. He held out his water bottle, clearing his throat when she continued forward, her eyes locked on the ground. She stumbled to a stop next to him, grabbing the bottle and lifting it over her head. The liquid poured out, splashing on her hair and running off to soak into the ground at her feet.

"You better hope we find more water soon," he grumbled, snatching his bottle back. "That was all I had left."

"Well, if Billy won't share, maybe she has some," April said, pointing ahead.

Simon spun around and gaped. The last thing he expected to find out in the woods was his high school girlfriend. His hand moved to the top of his head, patting at his thinning blond hair. *Why didn't I wear my cap?* Billy glanced back and offered him a wicked grin.

"Well holy shit," Billy called out. "If it's not the Pope Lick Princess."

Beth slid to a stop and frowned. Her eyes closed to slits, and Simon thought he could see waves of ice roll off the woman. Billy stepped closer, his laughter harsh and grating.

Simon sprang forward, hoping to defuse the situation. Billy was an acquired taste and one Beth was never a fan of.

"Nobody calls me that anymore, asshole," she growled through gritted teeth. Her hands balled into fists as Billy continued to approach her.

"That's right," Billy said with a bow. "We're not in school anymore, so there's no reason to stand on ceremony. Is there, your Highness? I mean ... for all anyone knows, you're just some dumb bitch that disappeared out in these woods."

April gasped.

"Okay," Simon started, hoping to calm the man down before he did something none of them could come back from. "Just keep ca—"

Beth stepped forward, driving her fist into Billy's nose with a sickening crunch. He cried out in pain, and his head shot back, blood gushing out and splattering to the ground. She kicked out, letting her foot sail up between his legs. He grunted and dropped to his knees with a whimper. Planting her feet, she pulled her arm back.

"Whoa," Simon called out, jumping between the two. "Beth ... stop. He's an asshole, but that's enough."

She blinked at him in confusion for a moment, then recognition dawned, and her arm dropped. "Jesus, Simon. What the fuck?"

April rushed forward and threw her arms around the woman. Laughter bubbled from the girl, and after a moment, Beth pulled back to study her. "Oh my God, look at you, honey. You gotta be breakin' hearts at Atherton High."

"She looks like a drowned rat," Simon said, still annoyed she wasted all his water.

Beth flashed him a disapproving glare and returned her attention to his sister, whose cheeks were now flushed in embarrassment. *Serves her right,* he thought with a smirk.

"What in God's name are you two doing out here with this asshole?" Beth asked, surprise heavy in her voice.

April glanced at her brother but remained silent. Beth's disapproving gaze fell on Simon, and after a moment, he shrugged. *She lost the right to question me years ago.*

"These two are helping me look for something," Billy grunted as he struggled to his feet. "Jesus, girl, ya pack a punch. I owe ya one."

Simon fished out a handkerchief from his pocket and handed it to the man. He nodded his thanks, his eyes locked on Beth. He wiped the blood from his face, smearing it across his lips.

"Oh, fuck off," she said, a smile on her lips. "You had that coming for a while now. You're just lucky Simon was here to save your ass. How about we call it even and someone gives me a working phone?"

April shook her head. "Simon and I don't have any reception. Our carrier sucks."

"And I left mine back in the truck," Billy barked out, pulling his water bottle free to wash the last bit of blood from his face. "Goddamn it, Beth. Ya ruined this shirt."

"I'll get you a new one, but first—"

Billy held up his hand. "Bullshit. There's no 'but first,' just fuck off." He stomped away.

Simon watched him disappear into the trees, then turned to Beth. "Ah shit, I'm sorry, but we need to catch up."

She reached out, grabbing his arm to stop him from leaving. With obvious concern in her eyes, she sighed. "I don't know what's going on, but I need your help. My friend fell and broke his leg. It's going to be dark soon, and I need to get him out of these woods."

"Simon, the right thing to do is to help Beth."

He stared at his sister. He couldn't remember the last time he let the right thing win out. Especially not since he teamed up with Billy. Her eyes widened a bit and darted towards Beth. A sly smile bloomed on her face, and Simon groaned.

"Not going to happen, kiddo."

"Really?" Beth asked, pressing her fists against her hips. "You're not going to help?"

"Not that," he said, waving his hand at them as he jogged after Billy. "Just give me a minute."

Simon found him just a few feet after the path disappeared from sight, hunched over with his arms wrapped around his belly. The scent of vomit hung in the air, and Simon grimaced.

"That bitch is going to pay," he growled, his eyes never leaving the ground.

"Sure, Billy," Simon said, stepping back to avoid the mess. "But now's not the time. Help me get her and her friend out of here so we can get back to searching for that weed Jay swears is out here."

"Jay wouldn't make that up," Billy said, straightening to take a swig of water. He rinsed it around his mouth, spitting it out at Simon's feet. "Look at you … still jumping through hoops for that cheatin' bitch. Hell, she shows up and you're like a fuckin' puppy … ready to lick her hand and do whatever she commands."

Simon closed the space between them in a flash, his finger driving into Billy's chest. "Use your fucking head. The last thing we need is a bunch of good Samaritans roaming the fucking woods. We get them out, and then we're back to building the empire."

He pulled his hand away, vaguely gesturing towards the trees all around them. Billy stared at him a moment, then slowly nodded. They walked back, Simon a few feet ahead. Beth and April grew quiet as they appeared. He nodded to his sister. She clapped her hands and hugged Beth.

"Help has arrived," Simon said with a grin. "Let's go find your friend."

CHAPTER SIX

"I don't understand," Beth said, her voice growing more frantic with each word. "He should be right down there."

April darted to the edge, grabbing Beth's arm so she could lean over to look. "Are you sure?"

Beth nodded and pointed to a spot. Simon and Billy shared a look and stepped closer. She glanced back. "Right there, you can see the damage to those branches."

"I guess," Billy replied with a shrug.

Beth spun around, pulling April with her. "Fuck you," she snarled. "This here tells me we're in the right spot." She pulled free the handkerchief from where she'd tied it.

"Okay," Simon said, holding his hands up in surrender. "Maybe he wasn't as hurt as you thought?"

Beth locked eyes with him, hers shiny with unshed tears, and shook her head. She took a deep breath, worried her voice would fail if she spoke right away.

"Or he got tired of your bullshit," Billy said with a smirk.

"Jesus," Simon barked. "Enough already."

April leaned further out. Beth glowered at the men, knowing she was being unfair lumping them together but furious Simon was friends with the asshole.

"Hey, is that a bag?"

Beth turned her attention to April. "What?"

"Right there, I can see a backpack," she answered, pointing in excitement.

Simon stepped over and, after a moment, nodded.

"Yeah, I see it."

"And?" Billy snapped. "So, the asshole was so hellbent on getting away from the *princess* he left it."

Simon stared at the other man a moment, the tension building in the silence. "Billy, get the Goddamn rope out," Simon said, his voice suddenly ice.

A chill ran through Beth, and she turned to study him. *What happened to the sweet boy I used to know?* Judging from his expression, she decided Billy must be thinking the same thing. He dug out a bundle of thick corded rope from his pack. Simon grabbed it and stepped to the closest tree. He wrapped the rope around it a few times, securing it with a complicated knot. He tested it with three quick tugs and walked back to the edge.

"I'm going to go down, and then, Beth, if you could send April before following, we can do a proper search. Billy, you need to stay up here to help anchor the rope. Got it?"

He held Billy's gaze until the man nodded. He wrapped the rope around his waist and stepped off the edge. Beth rushed over, amazed to see Simon already halfway down. He landed with a grunt, let the rope go, and stepped over to the tree that held the bag.

April grabbed the rope and followed her brother down. Beth glanced back at Billy, painfully aware they were alone. He dropped the rope and pulled out a knife from behind his back. He flashed a wicked smile and stepped towards her. The sunlight reflected off the blade, blinding her for a moment. Then he was beside her, his hand gripping her wrist tight.

"Since your dumbass boyfriend is gone, the best answer to our conundrum is becoming obvious," he snarled, pressing the edge against her throat. "Unless, of course, you want to convince me that won't be necessary."

Beth could feel his erection pressing against her leg as he pulled her closer. He licked her face, running his flat tongue up her cheek. She gagged, jerked herself free, and tumbled over the edge with a cry. She shot out her arm, desperately searching for the rope, and grabbed it when it brushed against her hand. The rough material tore into her skin as she slid to a stop to dangle about halfway from the bottom.

"Enough wasting time, Simon," Billy hollered. "It's time to go."

Beth jerked as the rope went limp and slithered over the edge to follow her down. She screamed again, surprised to land in Simon's arms instead of crashing on the hard ground.

"Goddamn it!" Simon barked, setting her down on her feet before steadying her. "We'll go as soon as this is taken care of. If you don't want to help, we can meet back at the truck." He turned his attention to Beth. "Let's find your friend and get y'all out of—Oh man, April, get me the first aid kit."

He reached into Beth's front pocket, the fabric the only thing between her skin and his probing fingers. Her eyes opened wide as her breath caught for a moment. He pulled out the handkerchief and pressed it against her throat. A hot, coppery scent reached her nostrils. Her stomach rolled, and she wondered if she was about to vomit on him. Simon offered a crooked smile, reaching behind her to free her water bottle.

"Drink a little of this," he said, the warmth returning to his voice. "I don't think we need to stitch up the cut, but I do want to bandage it. Best look at your hand as well."

Taking a sip, she stared into his eyes and wondered what had happened these past five years. Something hard hid just beneath the surface, and while she was grateful for Simon's help, she couldn't help but be frightened by him. Beth flinched when he covered the cut with a band-aid. He smiled and then wrapped her hand with a cotton bandage before pressing it secure.

"There, good as new. Now let's go find this dude. He couldn't have gotten far with a broken leg."

Simon turned and stepped over to the spot where they thought Martin had landed. He squatted, reaching out to move some of the undergrowth around. Beth took a step, jerked back, and spun in a circle.

"Simon, where's your sister?"

CHAPTER SEVEN

Terri glanced at the passenger seat and smiled at her daughter sleeping. It was hard to believe Harper was heading off to London in the summer and then to college. *Where has the year gone?* She figured there would be plenty of time, but as it usually seemed to do, life got in the way. Thank God she was able to get a few days off so they could continue their tradition. It would be earlier than their traditional time, but she couldn't risk them missing it altogether.

Her throat tightened at the thought. Seven years ago, her Albert died, right before the family's annual camping trip. She almost canceled it but decided to honor his love of the woods with one last excursion. *That camping trip was the only thing that kept us sane,* she thought with a sad smile. It brought them closer to him and, more importantly, each other. And now, she wondered if this might be the last one. *Gonna have to make these three days memorable.*

"In one mile, take exit one-thirty-six for US Thirty-One West Bypass North towards Fort Knox," a slightly robotic female voice said from her phone.

Harper stirred with a groan. She stretched her arms towards the backseat, her back arching until it gave a satisfying pop. "How long was I asleep?"

"Sorry, I meant to turn that down until we got off the highway. I think you've been asleep for about an hour, so maybe forty minutes and our adventure begins."

Harper popped open the glove box. She shifted the loose papers, owner's manual, and ketchup packets around with an ever-deepening frown. "Where is it?" she muttered, the last word becoming a cry of triumph as she pulled out a package of granola bars. She tore open the end and slid out one of the bars to offer to her mother like a cigarette from a pack.

"Thanks, honey," Terri said, leaning over to grab it with her mouth. She held it there a moment, clamped between her teeth to let the hard bar soften.

Harper reached behind the driver's seat and pulled out a water bottle. She motioned toward her mother, who shook her head. "Suit yourself. So where are we going again?"

"You remember Lisa? Well, her dad owns some land out near Tioga Falls, and he said we could camp out there as long as we clean up before leaving. She said it's close to the trails but far enough away from the day-to-day traffic."

"That was nice of them," Harper said.

"Yeah, so get ready 'cause we're gonna pack a week's worth of stuff into the next couple of days."

After April set the first aid kit down, she decided to give her brother some space. She couldn't remember the last time his expression had grown as soft as when he laid eyes on Beth back on the trail. It reminded her of how he used to be—before he got mixed up with people like Billy. *Fucking Billy.* She pulled up, a smear of blood on the ground distracting her from her thoughts.

The grass lay flattened as if a heavy object had been dragged across it. Another bloody smear repeated a few feet from the first. April stepped quickly, finding a third, then a fourth, and, finally, a fifth before the grass gave way to stone. She glanced back, no longer able to see her brother or Beth. Her heart fluttered, and a sudden flash of fear ran through her, quickly turning to panic. She took a deep breath and let it out slowly. *Jesus, calm down. They're, like, twenty yards away.*

She took another deep breath and grumbled, "Stop acting like such a little kid."

April gave herself a stiff nod in agreement and continued forward. Small patches of grass and moss sprang over and through the rocky ground. The undergrowth and trees, once tightly bunched, began to thin out and offered her a natural path forward. More blood let her know she was still moving in the right direction.

She kept her eyes down, sweeping them back and forth, looking for more of Martin's blood.

April stepped off the path and into a clearing the size of her bedroom. Sunlight filtered through the thick branches above, plunging the area into shadows. The trees circled around her on either side before running into a large stone wall that towered above the green foliage. A jagged gash of black ran through the rock, and after staring at it for a few moments, she decided it was an opening. She knelt in the center of the clearing and dug into her backpack.

"Where is it?" she mumbled, shifting the bag's contents around. With a cry of triumph, she pulled out her flashlight and stood. Aiming it toward the crack, April clicked it on.

The light shined at the top, and she moved it slowly down. Something struck her cheek, and she slapped at it, feeling it smoosh under her hand. God, how she hated the bugs this time of year. There was a sudden flicker, and she held the light still a moment. The darkness seemed different, although April couldn't put her finger on why. Again, something struck her cheek, but she ignored it.

She moved the light back up at a slower pace, hoping to again catch whatever flickered. *There.* The light caught something for a moment, then darkness. She held the flashlight steady, unconsciously holding her breath at the same time. Her eyes grew larger while staring at the spot. She took a step forward, pausing a moment before taking another.

April grew lightheaded. *Breathe, idiot.* The thought roared in her head, but she ignored it. Instead, she stared at two large, shiny orbs. She struggled to place the color, thinking it might be a light green or murky orange. The center was black and rectangular. The orbs disappeared, only to return a moment later. *Are those eyes?*

A man's voice spoke. "Are you alone?"

"Martin?" she called out, the fear in her belly growing. "I'm a friend of Beth's. We're here to help."

He repeated the question. "Are you alone?"

The orbs disappeared again just as something struck the top of her head. Annoyed, she pulled her gaze from the opening and looked up. Her mouth slipped open, and her chest expanded with the sudden intake of breath. A red mass dangled overhead. It took her a moment to realize she was looking at a person. A person missing their skin. Another drop of blood fell from their fingertips, striking her on the forehead. Her eyes shifted, catching movement from the rock. The shadow stretched out from the gash.

Terror washed over April, and the flashlight slipped from her fingers, cracking open on the hard ground. She struggled to comprehend what now towered over her. It stood upright on thick, muscular legs covered in coarse, dark hair. Its torso and arms, while mostly hairless, were covered in thick smears of muck and gore. Her gaze swept up, taking in the hairy broad shoulders before freezing on its face.

The creature's head was like that of a goat. Her gaze shifted from the two long, curved horns growing from between the pointed ears on the top of its head to the wide eyes studying her. It blinked, and a smile broke the thing's snout into two, exposing rows of jagged, sharp teeth.

"Little rabbits shouldn't be out here all alone. It's not safe."

April's chest burned, and the breath she'd been holding rushed out in a hoarse scream.

CHAPTER EIGHT

"This has to be the way," Beth said, a step behind Simon as he marched ahead. She glanced around, noting the blood smears and crumpled grass. Her throat tightened. *What could possibly have made Martin put himself through this much pain?*

"What is she thinking?" Simon grumbled, obviously unaware of the trail of blood they followed.

"Most likely, she thought this was where Martin went," she replied, drawing next to him. "Look there, and there. It's blood. Fresh blood."

"Wait ... what?" He pulled up, staring at the last spot she pointed at. "Didn't you say he broke his leg? What in the hell made him think moving was a good idea?"

She offered a shrug when he glanced at her. "I have no idea. He was in way too much pain to stand, let alone walk."

A terrified shriek filled the air. The skin on her arms broke out into gooseflesh, and they locked wide eyes. The scream lasted for what seemed forever, then cut off abruptly.

"April," he said before rushing towards the scream.

Beth stood frozen. Something in the girl's cry made her blood run cold. *That scream was a warning.* Whatever they found up ahead wouldn't be good. Of that, she was sure. The icy knot grew larger in her belly. She closed her eyes. *You got her into this.* The thought sounded more like an accusation than a statement of fact.

"I know," she whispered. Desperate to fill the silence, she continued to speak to herself. "Stop being a pussy and move your ass."

Each word came louder and with more force until the last one exploded out and set her in motion. Her right foot seemingly moved on its own, and soon she was running to catch up to Simon.

Beth closed the gap between them and followed him into a clearing. It took her eyes a moment to adjust to the hazy shadows. Motion grabbed her attention, and she shifted her gaze to the stone wall across from them, where April hung limply from a filthy, muscular arm. Then she was gone.

"April!" Simon screamed, rushing towards the wall. "Beth, there's an opening."

Beth scrambled to April's backpack, sitting in the middle of the clearing, its contents flung around the ground. A shattered flashlight lay off to the side. She glanced toward Simon, who held his flashlight and was motioning her to follow. She moved to follow but hesitated when she noticed a smear of blood off to the side. Nothing made any sense, and she prayed the blood was Martin's, but it still didn't explain where he was or who had Simon's sister.

"Beth, come on," Simon barked from the darkness, his light flashing towards her.

She shook her head, unsure just how good an idea it would be to follow anything into the caves.

★★★

Terri hammered in the last stake. She stood and stepped back to admire her handiwork. They'd decided to set the tent up a few feet from the center of the clearing they found at the end of a dirt road. A firepit was already built right in front of an overturned log. It was the perfect combination of space and isolation. She turned her head when the Outback's hatch slammed shut.

Harper carried her bag and a pair of boots over to the log and sat. She rummaged around, pulling out a can of bug repellant, a protein bar, and a thick pair of socks. She slipped off her grey Keds, pulled on the socks, and started to spray her bare legs. Terri stepped over and turned slowly so her daughter could spray her as well.

"Thanks, honey," she said, taking the can to apply the repellant to her arms, neck, and face.

Harper stood, stomping her feet to settle her boots. She leaned over, adjusted the laces, and stomped once more.

Terri glanced up, her hand shielding her eyes. "I think we can get in a few hours of hiking if you're up to it. Lisa said we would be about fifteen minutes from the main trail. There are caves, a waterfall, and a ton of nature in every direction."

"Sounds good. Let me get the cinch sacks."

Terri nodded and began to gather some wood to lay in the firepit. She wanted everything set up in case they took longer than expected. The vehicle's horn honked once, and Harper held out her mother's neon green sack. She patted her front pocket. "I've got the keys."

"Thanks," she said, taking the sack from her daughter before stepping into the trees. She hoped it wouldn't be the end of their tradition, but either way, she planned on making the most of this trip.

CHAPTER NINE

Simon held his light still until Beth squeezed through the opening and slipped next to him. He glanced at her, shining the beam on the floor between them. "There are three tunnels. Do you have a light?"

"I'm not fucking splitting up if that's what you're askin'," she said, the exasperation clear in her voice.

"Of course not, but it would be easier if we could both see."

He waited a moment, and she fished out her phone. She swiped at the screen, then pressed the flashlight and shined it around. "Guess it's better than nothing. Still no reception."

He sighed. *Figured as much.* Phones rarely worked out in the forest. Why would the caves be better? He shined the light on the first opening, off to the right. They stepped closer, each moving their light back and forth, looking for clues.

"I don't see anything," she said with a huff.

"Yeah, it's almost too—" He froze except for his back straightening. Beth turned her light towards him, illuminating his face when he asked, "Did you hear that?"

She shook her head, staying quiet. Simon took a step to the left, then another, his head cocked to the side.

"Here," a tiny voice called from the darkness.

Simon shined his light down the tunnel and leaned forward. Beth shuffled next to him, trying to stay quiet as they both strained to hear.

"Here ... I'm here."

Simon blinked a few times. *Is that April?* It sounded like her, but it was so muted he couldn't be sure.

"I think that's her, " Beth whispered.

He glanced at Beth, and after a slight hesitation, he nodded. "Yeah. I mean, it has to be ... right?"

He stepped into the tunnel, his light only lasting a few feet before the darkness swallowed it up. He paused, waiting for his sister to speak again. Beth hovered behind him.

"Hurry."

His throat tightened at the fear in her voice. "Yeah, that's her. This way," he whispered over his shoulder. He hurried forward, the darkness still overpowering the flickering beam.

"I'm scared." April's voice echoed through the tunnel.

Simon sped up, ignoring Beth's cries as he pulled away. The light fell on grey stone. "What the hell?" He slid to a stop, reaching out to touch the stone.

A fist struck him in the back. "Asshole!" Beth barked before striking him again.

"It's a dead-end," he said, his voice growing more frantic with each word. "I mean, she has to be here." He swung the flashlight around, spinning to study the tunnel.

Beth copied him and, after a moment, stepped to the wall on their left. "Something weird here."

Simon turned and reached out to run his fingers across the shimmering stone. The wall buckled under his touch, and he probed the spot, working out in a circular motion.

"This ain't rock," he mumbled, jerking it back. A strip of tarp tore from the ceiling and fell to the ground, revealing an opening.

Beth leaned forward, the light from her phone struggling to pierce the darkness before them. A blast of wind exited through the opening, and her head shot back. She twisted away from Simon, retching from the sudden stench that appeared with the breeze.

"Jesus Christ," Simon grumbled, burying his face in the crook of his arm.

Beth rested her right arm against the wall to stay upright, the other wrapped around her stomach. Dry heaves racked her body as she struggled to regain composure. Simon ran his hand on her back, patting it a few times. She straightened, pausing long enough to run the back of her hand across her mouth.

"Help me," April called out, her voice clearer than before.

"She must be through here," Simon whispered. He forced himself to ignore the stench and slipped through the opening.

"There's a light up ahead," he called back over his shoulder.

He continued to swing the flashlight, glancing around as he passed through. Scratch marks covered the walls, and deep grooves were worn into the stone floor. He immediately regretted taking a short breath as he choked on the foul stench. Blinking through watering eyes, he pulled up as they came to the tunnel's exit.

"Holy shit, the smell," Beth grumbled from behind.

Simon could only nod, reluctant to open his mouth again. He stared into a large circular room. Shafts of light shined down from holes in the ceiling, offering a haphazardly hazy illumination to the area. He stepped forward, his ankle catching a thin wire that ran across the opening. Cans rattled together on the other side of the room, and somewhere deep within the darkness, more cans sounded.

"Fuck!" he barked.

He could only imagine who might have set up such a primitive yet effective alarm system. *Hopefully, it's one Pete set—* The thought slipped away when his light fell upon a table in the middle of the room. He froze when he realized a body lay on the tabletop.

"Is it April?" Beth asked, placing her hand on his back.

He took a breath, with instant regret, and moved toward the table. His sister's face came into focus as his light swept over her still form. Reaching out, his hand hovered above her shoulder for a few seconds, afraid to discover she was no longer with them. He choked back a sob when he noticed her chest rise and fall, and ran his hand over her hair. April's eyes popped open.

She trembled under his touch and stared toward the ceiling with wide, unblinking eyes.

"She can't see you," Beth murmured, slipping next to him to shine her failing light on his face.

April sprang up, bending at the waist to throw her arms around her brother, any words lost in hysterical sobs. He held her and made soothing noises. Beth stepped away, walking around the room. Simon slipped his arm under his sister's rear and lifted her from the table. She buried her face in his shoulder.

"Umm, I think these are human," Beth called out before a coughing fit overtook her.

The stench somehow grew stronger with every step he took towards Beth. He handed her his flashlight, unable to maneuver it while supporting his sister's full weight. Beth shined it on the pile of refuse on the floor. Scraps of clothing, bits of hair, and bone fragments lay on a greasy tarp. He tried to ignore the tiny movements the light caught within the pile. He was positive they had finally discovered where the stench was coming from.

"I don't know what the fuck is going on, but we need to leave," Beth said, spinning around. The light landed on the opening they used to enter the room. Her breath caught, and Simon turned. In the shadows of the tunnel's entrance stood a man. "Martin?" Beth asked, a quiver in her voice. "Oh, God, are you all right? How did you manage to get this far?"

The man grunted, gliding into the room. He moved with a sway that Simon found unsettling. *Like a cobra's dance.* Simon stepped back and twisted his head around, searching for another way out.

"Beth ... something's wrong."

"Oh my God," she whispered. "What is that?"

Simon froze, struggling to process what he was seeing. His eyes locked onto the giant creature stepping from the darkness. It gripped Martin's skin by the shoulders, holding it out like an artist inspecting his latest masterpiece. The loose and empty husk rippled with each step the creature took, and it studied them through the large black holes that had once been Martin's eyes.

"Silly rabbits," the creature said in a perfect mimic of April's voice. It lowered the skin to expose its massive goat-like head. A nasty smile broke across its snout, exposing gore-covered fangs. "I lured you here."

"Oh Jesus," Beth said, her hand moving to cover her mouth. "I said that to Martin … just before the accident."

April clung to Simon, her face pressed so tightly against him that he wondered how she could breathe. He started to back away. Beth stood frozen, unable to take her eyes off the grotesque figure advancing toward them. He glanced backward, first over his left, then his right shoulder.

"Beth, shine the light just behind me," he cried out, shuffling in that direction. "NOW!"

His loud voice jolted Beth into motion, and her arm swung in that direction. It showed another opening and what Simon hoped was a way out of the caves. He turned, his sister hugged tight against him, and started to run. Bursts of laughter echoed through the chamber, and if he wasn't holding her tight against his chest, he would have sworn it came from his sister.

CHAPTER TEN

Tristan woke to the sound of his phone ringing. He turned his head to check the time. Twelve o'clock blinked back at him, letting him know he lost power at some point during the night.

"Damn it," he mumbled, shocked his mom hadn't woken him up before heading off to work. He grabbed his phone and swiped to answer. "Hello?"

"Hey, it's Billy. You got any plans today?"

"Hey, man." Tristan sat up and rubbed the sleep from his eyes. "Nah, whatcha need?"

"You did such a good job the other night, I wondered if you might be ready for more."

"One hundred percent," Tristan said without hesitation. "Whatever you need."

"Perfect. Did Simon ever introduce you to those two assholes of his, Mike and Lenny?"

"Yeah, I know them."

"Even better," Billy said. "Go round 'em up and bring 'em here. I'll text you the location."

The line went dead, and Tristan set the phone down. He shuffled to the bathroom and, after taking a long piss, turned on the shower. He smiled at his reflection. *Hot damn, the big man called me directly.*

Beth watched Simon run away as the laughter filled her ears. Her head swung back to the creature, and when her eyes locked onto Martin's flat face, she had a sudden urge to go to the bathroom. She wanted nothing more than to follow Simon, but instead, she stood frozen.

The Goatman flung the skin at the wall, where it struck with a wet *thwack*. It hung for a moment before gravity pulled at it, leaving a grotesque expression of horror upon Martin's lifeless visage. The creature stepped into the light, and Beth began to tremble. She studied the beast, her eyes taking in its cloven hooves and hairy, muscular legs. Her breath caught when her eyes fell upon the thick, veiny member hanging freely from the dark matted hair that grew up to its belly button.

Beth forced her eyes to continue up, noting the gunk and gore smeared all over the smooth, white skin of its torso. She stopped at its face and whimpered. Its mouth opened wide, with lips pulled back into a grotesque smile. Its head tilted, the large eyes studying her. Her bladder released, the hot urine soaking through her panties and shorts before running down her legs to pool beneath her.

The Goatman began to sniff the air, its head moving back and forth with each intake. She wondered how it could smell anything other than the stench of death that hung in the room.

"Time to run," it said in Simon's voice, pausing a moment before screaming, "NOW!"

Beth jerked into motion, spinning and rushing to follow the others into the tunnel. The Goatman began to laugh once again, and the eerie sound chased Beth into the darkness.

CHAPTER ELEVEN

April clung to Simon, whimpering between choked sobs. He struggled to keep his balance as he raced blindly through the tunnel. He glanced over his shoulder, trying to make sense of the odd laughter echoing around them. It seemed to shift back and forth between a grown man and his sister. *What is going on?* The flashlight beam popped into view, and soon Beth was behind him, pressing her hand into his back.

"Faster," she cried out. "It's right behind us."

Simon turned sideways, pressing against the wall so she could slide by. "It'll be easier if you light the way."

The laughter grew closer, and heavy steps echoed through the tunnel. He rushed to keep up with Beth, his eyes locked on the bobbing beam of light. A dull ache ran through his back and up his arms, his sister growing heavier with each step.

"April," he said through gritted teeth. "Can you walk? I'm about to drop you."

With a whimper, her fingers dug deeper, and he winced, surprised by their strength. Simon stumbled, his feet slipping out from under him. He twisted his body, and she tumbled from his grip with a startled cry. Beth turned, shining the light on the siblings as they crashed to the stone floor.

"Jesus. Are you guys all right?"

Sobbing, April curled into a ball. Beth knelt and placed her hand on the girl's back. With a groan, Simon pushed up from the ground. Holding his side, he struggled to catch his breath, each attempt sending a burst of pain through his ribs. Beth gasped; her hands clawed at April, pulling the girl into her arms. She swung the flashlight up and blinded Simon. He blinked away the stars, flinching at the women's sudden wails of terror. Fingers gripped his hair, pulling his head back until his spine creaked from the pressure.

His vision cleared, and he found the face of the Goatman staring down at him. A glob of drool hung from the corner of the creature's lips. Simon locked onto it as it grew longer and dangled over him. His ears rang as their cries bounced off the walls of the tunnel. The beam of light shifted a bit, and Simon's attention jumped from the slobber to the flash of metal hovering over the Goatman's head. *Is that an ax?*

★★★

Billy glanced at the rearview mirror, studying the three men sitting in the bed of his truck. *God damn bottom of the barrel*, he thought with a shake of his head.

"Fuck me," he groaned, wincing from the jolt of pain shooting through his nose. "Ugh, if I ever get my hands on that bitch ..."

He trailed off, finding no pleasure in imagining what he'd do. This wasn't about his nose. A phantom ache in his crotch pulled his attention down. *Or you.* He grimaced, remembering the sharp pain as her foot drove into his boys. While he would enjoy paying her back for both offenses, it was Simon's betrayal that demanded a reckoning. *The Pope Lick Princess bats her fucking eyes in that asshole's direction, and he drops everything.* He checked his phone, but there were no missed calls. *Still trying to get his dick wet instead of takin' care of business.*

And while he was confident he knew what was occupying Simon's attention, something about Jay's disappearing was off. Even if he couldn't build up the nerve to off Pete in the caves, he wasn't the type of person to run. *Unless those two went Brokeback all the sudden.* No matter what, it left Billy without the exact location of the caves or the weed Jay swore was growing out there. He punched the steering wheel in frustration. Somewhere out there was his base of operations, and it was going to take some kind of hillbilly voodoo to find it. He glanced back at the rearview mirror and sighed.

That or a shit ton of luck. The plan was simple. He had a general idea of where the cave was, and the four of them would start there. While he always expected they would need to expand at some point, Simon and Jay pulling disappearing acts forced his hand. He had no choice but to bring Mike, Lenny, and Tristan into the fold. All that mattered was finding the cave and the weed. Four pairs of eyes were better than one, plus he wasn't about to go traipsing around the fucking woods alone. What if those two fucknuts were actually looking to cut him out? He would need the backup.

Billy exited the highway and drove until they came to a small dirt road that disappeared into the woods. He stopped and rolled down his window. "Hold on, fuckers … ride's about to get bumpy."

He gunned the truck, knocking up a cloud of dust that settled on the three in the back. Billy smiled as he watched them choke in the rearview mirror. Maybe losing Simon wasn't the worst thing. He shifted his gaze to study his reflection. Now there would be no question about who was in charge.

CHAPTER TWELVE

Beth screamed when the trembling flashlight beam illuminated the Goatman standing over Simon. It gripped the man by his hair, jerking his head back to expose his neck. It held an ax above its head, but she couldn't pull her gaze away from the long string of saliva that dangled from the creature's mouth. Her cry cut off just long enough to take a deep breath to begin anew.

The drool broke free, splattering onto Simon's cheek a moment before the ax's blade sliced through his neck. Blood spurted out, spraying the Goatman in gore before the body tumbled to the stone floor. It held Simon's head up, placing it directly in front of the light, and bursts of giggles filled the tunnel, growing in volume until they drowned out the women's screams. The Goatman tossed Simon's head, bouncing it off April's chest to land on the ground at her feet.

April's scream cut short, and vomit spilled from her mouth, splashing over her brother's face. Beth grabbed the girl's arm and jerked her back. The Goatman stepped towards them, its laughter dying down to a wheeze. Beth's hand slipped down April's arm, interlocking her fingers with the girl's, and they ran.

"Come back," Simon's voice sounded from behind. A chill ran through Beth. *It's not him.* "Don't leave me."

It's not him. The urge to stop, turn, and go back suddenly overwhelmed her, and she slowed to a brisk walk.

"Why are we slowing down?" April asked, her voice a whisper.

"I ... don't ... know," she answered, her voice reflecting her own confusion. "Your brother needs help."

"He's fuckin' dead. Just like the skinned guy." The words sounded harsh to Beth's ears, but the image of Martin's skin being held out for them to see flashed in her head.

"Jesus ... you're right," she mumbled with a sob.

She picked up her pace, pulling April along as they began to run once again. Laughter and heavy footsteps echoed after them. Beth swung the flashlight back and forth, frantically searching for any way out of the tunnel. *What was that?* She stopped, spinning around to shine the light back on the wall. *There, just like before.* She held the flashlight steady and leaned closer.

"Come on!" April cried out, hopping back and forth. "Goddamn it, that thing killed my brother, and we're next if you don't move."

Beth froze; a twinge of guilt flashed through her. *They're both dead because of me.* A lump formed in her throat at the thought. *I just had to go hiking.* But how could she have known there was something like that monster out here? She shook her head and reached out to the wall.

"I think there might be a way out," she said, trying to interject some hope into her voice.

April ran back to Beth and snatched the flashlight out of her hand. "That thing is gonna be here any minute, so we need to be gone."

The tunnel fell back into darkness as the girl ran further away. "God damn it." Beth pressed her hand to the wall, sighing when it buckled inward. She gripped it and pulled to reveal an opening. Hazy light filtered down from the ceiling on the other side. It appeared to be a room, but she thought there might be an exit on the far wall. The echo of cans rattling from somewhere in the darkness and April's sudden scream pulled her attention back. There was no sign of the flashlight, and for a moment, she wondered if she shouldn't stay put. Then the guilt returned, and she slapped her hand against the stone. She walked in the direction April had run, using the wall as a guide.

After a few feet, Beth could hear some noises. She struggled to make them out: wood knocking, a constant gurgling hiss, and the occasional high-pitched whine mixed in. The flashlight beam came into view; it spun in a slow circle. A thin line of white ran across the tunnel, appearing and disappearing as the light passed by. She stopped short, noting it was at ankle level before stepping over it to grab the flashlight.

She trained the light on the hole in the center of the tunnel's floor. April came into view. She seemed to be floating in the darkness, but after a moment, Beth saw the wooden spikes driven through her left cheek, shoulder, back, and right leg. She squirmed, each movement knocking some of the spikes against the stone wall.

"Heeeaaappp," she moaned, the thick shaft of wood in her mouth muffling her cry for help.

Beth stared at the girl.

What can I do? Her head shot up. Heavy footsteps echoed through the tunnel.

"Dooonnn' leeeavvee," April cried out, the second word shifting to a sob.

A rumble sounded from somewhere within the rock, and strings of dingy lightbulbs flickered to life. The footsteps grew closer, and Beth turned in a tight circle, desperate to find a place to hide. The flashlight beam fell on a crevice in the wall. She hurried to it and crawled into the opening. It went back a few feet, and when she pulled her legs to her chest, she fit perfectly in the tiny hole.

Beth turned off the flashlight and waited. Her stomach rolled as the click-clack steps echoed through the tunnel. She slammed her eyes closed but, after a moment, opened them enough to peek out. The Goatman appeared and stepped past her hiding spot. The creature made its way to the trap and studied April as her sobs shifted back to cries of terror.

"Nooooooo," she howled, the word seemingly building in volume within the tunnel. "Heeeaaappp, Beeeppppffff."

Beth gently touched her cheek, imagining what it would be like to have that stake driven through it, as she listened to the poor girl call out her name. *The pain must be incredible.* A single tear slipped from her right eye and slid down her cheek.

She forced her attention back to the trap and the Goatman. It squatted down and reached into the hole. April's screams increased in volume, and Beth's throat tightened at the wet suction sound of the girl being pulled free from the wooden stakes. The Goatman stood up and held April by her throat.

April clawed at its wrist, struggling to free herself from its iron grip. Tiny whimpers replaced her screams as she fought for breath. Beth's gaze locked on the girl's feet, and a sense of melancholy settled over her.

April's legs kicked about but slowed with each passing second until they hung loosely with only an occasional twitch. The Goatman reached out and grabbed her arm with its free hand. Beth sat wide-eyed, struggling to process what was happening before her.

"I met a girl in these hills," the Goatman sang tunelessly, its voice no longer one she recognized but that of an older woman, full of regret and sorrow. With a sigh, the creature continued. "And I needed to know what to do. My mother handed me a rose and said the answer was in the petals."

Beth stared, unable to tear her eyes away. Without warning, it tore April's arm off at the shoulder socket.

"She loves me."

Beth slapped her hand over her mouth, desperate to trap the cry building in her chest. The Goatman tossed the arm back into the hole and moved to the next one. "She loves me not." Blood spurted from the jagged wound, and the creature dropped that arm into the hole as well.

April's eyes rolled into her head, and her body went slack. Blood flowed from the stumps and ran down her sides to splash into the hole. The Goatman began to cackle, the laughter coming out in bursts like gunfire. Beth's skin crawled at the sound, and she hugged her legs tighter. April's eyes shot open, and she offered a whimper. The muscles in the beast's arm flexed, and its grip tightened on her throat. It grabbed her leg and, with a sudden explosion of movement, tore April's head from her neck.

"SHE LOVES ME."

Blood squirted up, spraying the ceiling, and then gushed out of the stump to splash onto the stone floor. Vomit sprayed through Beth's fingers, and her sphincter tightened as her bowels threatened to release. The Goatman continued to giggle and dropped the body into the hole. Its head shot back, and it took a few deep sniffs.

Beth closed her eyes and began to silently pray. A strong musky scent overwhelmed her, overtaking the odor of her filth soaking into her clothes. She snuck a peek but saw only darkness. Her chest tightened, and she struggled to find her breath. *Did the lights go out?* She pulled the flashlight from her side and struggled with the switch, her vomit making it slippery. It finally clicked on, and her face blanched as the Goatman's hairy groin appeared.

The creature squatted down, its eyes closed tight. Her light illuminated a broad, hideous smile while drool spilled from the corners of its mouth. It ran its tongue across its bottom lip, and the creature's eyes popped open.

"Peek-a-boo," it said with a giggle, reaching in to grab her by the ankle. "I found you."

The flashlight flickered off, and Beth began to scream.

CHAPTER THIRTEEN

Scott gasped for breath. His legs burned with each step, and he wondered how he was gonna survive five days of this. His gaze fell onto Amber's ass. *Oh yeah.* She was a few yards ahead, her long legs eating up the ground with each step. She hadn't even begun to run, saying she was going to take it easy on him for the first day or so. His foot came down on a rock, twisting his leg when it shifted and sending him to the ground.

"Fuck," he cried out, landing on the trail with a grunt. His palms stung from breaking his fall, but his thoughts were all on his knee.

He rolled to rest on his backside, gingerly pulling up his leg so he could inspect the brace. A flash of pain ran up his thigh but quickly subsided as he clenched his jaw.

"Scott, you all right?"

He glanced up, forcing his grimace into a smile. "Yeah, babe, just tripped." She raised an eyebrow, and his smile widened. "Really, I'm fine ..." He trailed off. His focus shifted from her disapproving face to the line of trees just a few feet behind her. He couldn't put his finger on why he thought they were being watched, but he was sure of it. His skin crawled, a sense of dread filling his belly.

Amber studied him for a moment before glancing around. "What?" she said, studying the trees.

"I think some ... thing's out there."

"Yeah, it's the woods. Things live out here," she said, her smile returning as she walked back to him.

He sighed, and with the sensation now gone, he focused on her swaying towards him. She squatted and reached out to place her hand on his cheek before leaning in to kiss him. It started off soft but hinted at things to come, and he decided he was ready to get a move on, if only to make it to the campsite quicker.

She patted his cheek before standing. "Sorry about the pace. I forgot what a little bitch you are. Do I need to kiss your boo-boo, or can we get back to it?"

Scott laughed, and the last bit of tension drained from his shoulders. "Yes, but to be completely transparent, I landed on my dick when I fell."

Amber rolled her eyes and held out her hand. He grabbed it and let her help him to his feet. He took a few steps, leaning this way and that, happy to see nothing in his knee hurt. *Thank God for the brace.* She wrapped her arms around his waist and pulled him closer. They kissed, and she increased the pressure until his lips opened slightly so her tongue could slip into his mouth.

Scott slid his hands down her back, grabbing and squeezing her ass. He started to grow hard as their bodies pressed together. Amber pushed against his chest, breaking their kiss. Panting, she offered a grin. "Better slow down, cowboy, we've still got a ways to go, but play your cards right ..." She grabbed his erection and slid her hand up and down over his shorts.

He snatched her wrist and pulled her hand away, a look of consternation on his face. "I'd rather not walk around with crusty drawers if I can help it. At least not on the first day."

She giggled and leaned close enough to give him a peck on the lips. "We find a good campsite and crusty drawers will be the last thing on your mind. Now let's get that knee moving again."

Scott groaned as he shifted the pack on his shoulders and hurried to keep up.

***

"Holy shit," Mike said from the tree line. "We almost got a show. What I wouldn't give to see those titties up close."

Lenny grinned, his head nodding in agreement. He looked at Tristan, who offered a shrug. "Yeah, she was ah'right."

Mike slung his arm around Lenny's shoulder and laughed. "You listenin' to this mother fucker? *Ah'right*, my ass. That fine ass bitch is in heat, and we could be the ones to help her scratch that itch."

"The only thing you assholes need to be helping is me find the weed and the cave," Billy barked, stepping back from the tree he was just pissing against. He stuffed his dick back into his pants and wiped his hands on his jeans. "I've already lost Simon and at least a week's worth of profit because of some twat out in these woods."

"Don't forget your sense of smell too," Mike said, his grin growing with each word.

Billy rushed forward, jamming his forearm against Mike's throat as he slammed the man against a tree. "Listen, 'cause I'm only going to say it once. You fuckers are lucky I'm giving y'all another chance, and if you can keep your shit together, we all are gonna be swimming in green. Simon decided to chase after some pussy, and I let his sorry ass go without batting an eye ... and I like Simon."

He pulled away, spun around, and stomped from the three stunned men. Mike rubbed his throat, clearing it several times to no avail. *Fucker almost crushed it.*

"We better catch up," Tristan said over his shoulder as he moved to follow Billy.

Mike spit off to the side and said in a hoarse whisper, "Shame if something happened to that motherfucker right after we find the goods. Whatcha ya think about that?"

Lenny ran his thumb across his throat.

"That's what I'm talking about," Mike said with a hoot.

INTERLUDE TWO

"Please ... are you there? I promise I won't tell. Just let me go. Please ... It's so dark ... PLEASE."

CHAPTER FOURTEEN

Terri took a long drink from her water bottle. It was hotter than she expected it to be this time of year. *Be nice once we get to the waterfall, hopefully.*

Harper stopped walking. "You comin'?"

"Yeah, I guess I'm more out of shape than I thought," she replied, struggling to slip the bottle back into her cinch sack.

Harper looked back, making a show of rolling her eyes. "I hope to be that 'out of shape' when I'm thirty, let alone forty-three."

Terri walked to her daughter and threw her arms around her to pull her in for a tight hug. She kissed her on the cheek. "Well, thank you kindly. I don't believe ya ... but it was nice to hear."

"Gross, you're sweaty."

She let her daughter push her away without too much of a struggle. They walked in silence, enjoying the peace of the woods. *Will this be our last one?* Her eyes shone with emotion, and though she hoped it would continue, she wasn't sure now that her daughter was grown.

Harper reached over and took her hand. "Mom, promise me we won't stop doing this," she said suddenly. "Please remind me that I want ... no, need to do this."

Terri squeezed her hand and forced a laugh out to clear her throat. "Well, sure, honey. If it's that important to you, I'm sure I can make the time."

The trees began to crowd the path, offering shade. They continued to walk, pausing to listen to the birds sing or the squirrels chatter in the treetops or point out all the things Albert would have liked. They stepped from the path onto a strip of grass that ran into a stretch of gravel. Railroad tracks sat over the rocks, one way stretching until it disappeared on the horizon, the other quickly running from the ground to a bridge and then disappearing back into the woods.

Harper pulled free and rushed to the edge of the cliff and looked down. "Jesus, Mom. It's, like, thirty feet down."

"Well, don't fall."

She glanced back and stuck her tongue out. "Thanks."

"Come on. I'm pretty sure if we cut across here and follow the tracks a bit, we can find that waterfall I was telling you about."

Harper hesitated, continuing to stare down. Terri pulled away, walking next to the tracks on the gravel. She turned when a loud horn sounded in the distance. Her foot came down awkwardly, and she tumbled backward, her arms flailing.

"Mom!"

The horn sounded again. *Man, that sounds close.* The thought was driven from her head as it struck the edge of the track. She blinked away the stars and struggled to regain the breath the fall knocked from her body. The ground rumbled and shook, and a loud roar drowned out Harper's cry. She wanted to move but instead continued to simply lay on the ground. Her eyes grew unfocused, and the bright sun began to fade. Fingers wrapped around her wrist, and Harper dragged her over the gravel until only soft grass was beneath her. Water splashed on her face, wetting her lips and shocking her eyes open.

Harper stared down, concern in her eyes. "Thank God."

The train whooshed by with the horn still blaring, and Terri imagined if she looked over, there would be a conductor shaking his fist at her. *Oh well.* She struggled to sit up. Harper gently poked and prodded around her scalp, looking for any serious injuries. Terri reached up and pointed to where it hurt.

"Oh, man," Harper groaned. "You're going to have a lump the size of a golf ball … but no blood." She poured some water on the spot and held the bottle out for Terri to take.

Terri drank it all and sighed. "Thanks, honey. We can get me cleaned up at the waterfall. We didn't come this far just to turn back now."

Harper stared at her, her face blank. Then she sighed and offered her hand to help her mother stand. Terri got to her feet, swayed a moment, and then, after a step or two, declared she was fine.

The women started to walk along the tracks, Harper keeping them both on the grass. Terri glanced over and smiled. She wrapped her arm around her daughter's shoulder and squeezed. "Seriously, I'm okay. Nothing is going to ruin this trip."

CHAPTER FIFTEEN

Amber turned around and frowned when she saw Scott bent over, his hands fiddling with his brace again. She bit her bottom lip. They should have ignored the gas station guy and kept to the plan. Instead, they were having to constantly stop during the hike, and there was no place to legally camp. While she enjoyed Scott's mischievous grin when he told her that would make the trip more exciting, she doubted getting shot at by some pissed-off farmer was going to add any extra thrills to their relationship. That said, she was ready for some alone time in their tent.

"You okay?" she called out, walking back to where he stopped.

"Yeah, something was rubbing against my knee. Just making an adjustment. I sure hope I don't have to wear this on the mound."

Scott straightened, and Amber could see the worry in his dark green eyes. His cheeks colored, and he pulled his ballcap off to run his hands through his sandy-blond hair before putting the cap on backward. *My kryptonite*, she thought with a smile and reached out to take his hand.

"Honey, you have to give it time to heal," she said, her voice soft and steady. "But if you have to wear the brace, you'll wear the brace and continue to dominate. There's no doubt in my mind."

"You know that weirdo at the gas station asked me how I got so lucky," he said, leaning in to give her a quick kiss.

She reached around and grabbed his ass. "Who says I'm not the lucky one?"

"Everyone," he replied with a laugh.

She took his hand, and they began to walk in silence. She fought the urge to rush ahead, instead glancing around to take in the nature around them. The trail was cleared of any undergrowth, but a few steps off the path in any direction and they would disappear into the wilderness. The trees towered over them, and sunlight filtered down through the branches. Even with the occasional bird crying out, she found the steady hum of nature soothing.

"Is that a mailbox?" Scott asked with a laugh.

Amber turned her head, following where he pointed. The woods opened up, and the path became more of a road. Sitting off to the side was a large mailbox shaped like a church. She pulled her hand free and circled around it, taking in the details. It was one-story, with a large, slanted roof and a steeple sticking up at the front. River of Life Church and a faded address was stenciled on the side.

Dropping her pack, she pulled out her phone and held it out. "There might not be any service out here, but you can still take my picture." She draped her arm over the top and leaned against the box. Scott took a few shots, checking each one before continuing. *Got him trained.* Her smile widened at the thought.

"Wonder if anything is in there," he said reaching out to grab the handle on the front. He held out the phone and, with his eyebrows raised, asked, "You want to narrate for the big reveal?"

Amber grabbed the phone and switched to video. She stepped off to the side of Scott and started. "Today in Weird Shit in the Forest, we have a miniature church. When we open it up, will we find tiny parishioners, the souls of the damned, or a letter from Publishing Clearing House?"

Scott took a deep breath and pulled. "Huh."

"Well, that was a bit of a letdown," Amber said after a long pause. "I guess it's the Capone Vault of mailboxes." She pocketed her phone and stepped back. Her eyes drew back to the box as a humming buzz began to sound.

"Oh shit," Scott yelped, slamming the box shut. He hopped back, his head moving back and forth. "Watch out, babe. You need to move."

Amber let loose a squeak and took off. Scott glanced back and sighed. *Well ... shit.* He snatched up her pack but kept his eyes on the angry insects. Once he felt confident the wasps weren't going to follow, he turned and started to run. Even at full strength, he never could keep up with her. *No chance now*, he thought. She would do anything to avoid being stung this far away from a hospital, no matter how many epi-pens she had in her bag.

"Hey, wait up," he called out, praying she just slowed down a little. He might have had a chance if she still had her pack, but since he had them both, he gave up after a few yards and slowed to a fast walk. He'd either catch up eventually or she'd come back.

Hopefully.

CHAPTER SIXTEEN

Billy walked a few feet behind Mike and Lenny, letting them clear the way. He glanced at Tristan, who strode next to him, and frowned. *What is this world coming to?* From day one, the man had rubbed him the wrong way, but because Simon vouched for him, Billy gave him a chance. His jaw clenched. *And now this dumbass is gonna replace him ... Goddamn it, Simon.*

"With Simon pulling this bullshit, I'm gonna need someone a bit more standup," he said, his voice low enough to keep the conversation between just the two of them. "You know someone that fits that description?"

The two men walked in silence, the only noise the sound of the machetes chopping the vegetation ahead. Tristan nodded and offered a crooked grin. "I mean, if you're asking me to step up, I'm all in. Simon's my friend, but this is business and he did you wrong."

"Good man," Billy said, punching him in the arm. "When we get back, we can go over the deets."

"Yes, sir," he said, pulling up. "The wonder twins have stopped."

Billy laughed, turning his attention to the men standing next to each other, gasping for breath. "What's the matter, boys?" he asked, stepping between them.

They were at the top of a rise, and below them, a train track ran through an open stretch of land. *Now who are these bitches?* Two women walked hand in hand parallel to the tracks. He guessed they were family and, after a moment, settled them being mother and daughter. He glanced at the men and sighed. If he didn't play it right, there'd be a mutiny. *Fucking Simon all over again, goddamn it.* He could bully them past one girl, but it would be hard with those two down there just asking for it.

"Let me guess; you boys want to play."

Mike leered at the women, holding his machete like a giant metal dick and thrusting towards them. Lenny nodded with a wide grin splitting his face.

"How do you know they're alone?" he asked, glancing at each man.

"We could follow them a bit, and if no one shows up ..." Mike shrugged, letting the unspoken threat hang between them.

"They are walking in the same direction we're going," Tristan said, stepping next to Lenny to watch the women walk away.

Billy took a deep breath. "Fine, since we're going the same way. We can keep an eye on them, and at the falls, we'll reassess."

Mike hooted and held out his hand for Lenny to high-five. "I told you it wouldn't hurt to ask."

CHAPTER SEVENTEEN

"Oh wow," Terri said, clapping her hands. "It's beautiful."

The two women stood at the base of Tioga Falls, a series of rock shelves that ended with a ten-foot waterfall drop. Water cascaded from the edge, striking the earth and rolling away in small streams. They placed their sacks off to the side, away from the water, and stepped closer to the waterfall.

"Watch your step," Harper called out, hoping her mom heard her over the water's rush.

Terri nodded, flashing her a smile before sliding closer. Harper followed a step behind, ready to spring if her mother should stumble. The water splashed on them, soaking their legs. *Oh, that feels so good.* The roar of the water swallowed up her mother's laughter as she stepped under the downpour and began to gently probe her scalp

"This does help," she called out.

Harper nodded and smiled. She stuck her hands out, letting the water rush over her fingers. It was cool and refreshing after their long hike. *Bet it's great in August ... if there's still water.* She pulled the tie from her ponytail and shook her hair loose before leaning forward to let the water stream over her head. She gasped, the water suddenly feeling much colder than before.

"Well, what do we have here, boys?" a man called out.

Harper pulled her head back and wiped at her eyes before spinning around. Her mother moved closer, her arm sweeping out to steer Harper behind her. Four men stood a few yards away, spread out so there was no clear escape for the two women. *Oh shit.*

The biggest man she had ever seen leaned over and scooped up their bags. He looked in both, shook his head, and glanced over to a man who could only be described as his opposite. "I don't see any towels in here, Lenny."

Lenny smiled back and offered a shrug.

"Shit, Mike. No names," the third man said, a grimace on his lips.

Harper knew his type, some rich douche who thought hanging out with dangerous folks gave him some sort of street cred. God, she hated those assholes.

"Well hot damn, *Tristan*," Mike said as he dropped the sacks. "That's a mighty fine idea."

Mike and Lenny advanced, and after a moment's hesitation, Tristan followed. The fourth man hung back. He seemed disinterested in the events transpiring, and Harper wondered if his recently broken nose had anything to do with it.

"Now, boys," Terri said, her voice strong and steady. "People know we are out here."

She stepped back, forcing Harper to move closer to the waterfall.

"Oh, that's fine," Mike said with a wide, friendly smile. "'Cause no one knows we are."

Lenny offered a snicker and clapped his hands.

"We don't have all day," the fourth man called out. Harper watched him sit down on a dry log.

"You heard the boss," Mike said, stopping to tower over the women. "We are on a bit of a time crunch. So, I'm going to give you a choice." He leaned over, sighing from the effort, and put himself eye-to-eye with Terri. "You can *both* get to suckin', or me and the boys will use you like a Chinese finger cuff."

Harper grabbed her mother's shoulder. She stared at the man's face, repulsed by the lust burning in his eyes. Lenny slipped closer, his hands reaching out to cup Terri's breasts through her shirt. Harper felt her mother go rigid at the touch, and she slapped away the skinny man's hands. He pulled back with a giggle.

"Looks like your girl's made the decision," Mike said as he straightened. His hand began to work on loosening his belt.

"NO ... no," Terri said, stepping forward. Her hands pushed past the man's finger to grip the belt buckle. "I'll do it. Just please ... leave her alone."

"I really want to," Mike said, his left hand running through Terri's short hair. "But my man here likes them a little bit younger than you. Maybe you can convince him he's wrong."

Harper surged forward, grabbing her mother and pulling her back. "Enough, you fucking assholes."

Tristan stomped over, grabbing Harper's arm to pull her from her mother. "Listen, cutie. I'm pretty sure she's about to be skewered, but if you treat me right, I promise you'll enjoy it."

Harper spat in his face. "Fuck you."

He slammed his fist into her stomach, knocking the air from her. She bent over and clutched her gut. "Yeah, bitch, that's exactly what's happening."

"No!" Terri cried out.

She tried to move to her daughter's side, but Mike grabbed her hair and jerked her back. He lifted her from the ground, her hands grabbing at his wrist as she rose higher. Lenny clawed at her shorts, his long, gunk-caked fingernails scratching her skin as he hooked her waistband. She screamed in frustration and began kicking her legs. Lenny only laughed as he slipped her shorts off and tossed them to the side.

Harper crumpled to her knees, struggling to find her breath. Tristan ran his fingers through her thick, black hair and made a fist. She cried out when he jerked her head back. "That's the spirit. I've always wanted to do one of you goth chicks. I've heard y'all are real wildcats when y'all get into it."

The pounding of her heart filled her ears, drowning out her mother's cries and the men's laughter. His grip tightened, and she winced as hairs tore from her scalp. Her eyes locked on his free hand undoing the button on his shorts before pulling the zipper down. He fished out his erection, waving it in front of her face. Harper glanced up, afraid to open her mouth to beg him to stop. Her stomach lurched at the eagerness shining in his eyes.

She saw his lips move, and though she couldn't hear him, she knew what he said. *Open up, bitch.* With a whimper, she closed her eyes and prayed it would be over soon.

CHAPTER EIGHTEEN

"Did you hear that?" Scott asked, his head cocked to the side.

Amber nodded with a frown. "Yeah ... that wasn't a bird, was it?"

Scott shook his head, speeding up to a jog. Amber stayed by his side a moment but accelerated when another scream came.

"Babe, slow down. Goddamn it."

He picked up his speed, ignoring the brace rubbing on his knee. Amber disappeared as the trail curved out of view. Scott glanced to the side, saw an opening between the trees, and entered the woods. He weaved through the foliage, searching for the clearest path. He hopped over a fallen tree, his foot landing on a patch of moss that sent him sprawling into a thicket of blackberry bushes.

"Shit," Scott yelped, struggling to pull himself free from the thorny branches.

Another scream sounded, and Scott closed his eyes. *No time for careful,* he thought before jerking back. The thorns tore from his flesh. He paused a moment to breathe through the sudden flash of pain. When his vision cleared, he found himself staring at a pile of round stones. *These will work.* He snatched up three of the rocks and hurried forward, handling each one in his right hand to get a feel for them. They were slightly smaller than the baseball he threw during a game, but each one was relatively smooth and circular. He came to the edge and slid to a stop. *What the fuck?*

Over to his left, right next to a waterfall, was a group of six people. He struggled to process what he was seeing: one man sat calmly on a log, a preppy douche was waving his hard-on in the face of a young woman, and a giant tub of lard held a tight grip on the hair of another woman Scott thought might be an older relative to the first woman. A skinny little dude was dancing about them, hooting and hollering and spinning the woman's panties on his upraised finger.

Each time the woman screamed, the men grew more excited. Scott gripped one rock, palming the other two in his left. He paused, but when no one noticed him, he continued forward. He opened his mouth to issue a warning but stopped when Amber burst from the side.

She ran to the edge and leaped towards the two men with the older woman. A primal scream ripped from her chest, and it was then he noticed the hatchet in her hand. She held it backward and struck the large man's arm with it as she landed. A loud snap echoed, and the woman slipped from his grasp, landing on her ass with a grunt. Scott's cheeks colored, his eyes falling on her dark, bushy mound exposed between her legs.

"You bitch!" the large man screamed, clutching his arm tight to his chest.

Amber kicked out and drove the heel of her boot into the skinny man's crotch with a loud crunch. He grabbed his groin and tumbled to the ground. The man on the log began to rise, his hand reaching into his waistband. Scott pulled his arm back, fired the rock across the way, and the man crumpled to the ground.

"Look out," Scott hollered, hoping to warn Amber of the large man rushing at her.

Scott ran towards the group, one of the remaining stones now in his throwing hand. He prayed Amber could hold off the brute for a moment longer, his attention now on the douchebag and the dark-haired girl. She lay on the ground, curled into a ball; the man stood there, his flaccid penis still resting in his hand. The rock exploded from Scott's hand, closing the distance in seconds. A sharp crack sounded, and the man dropped next to his victim.

He shifted his attention back to Amber, happy to see her dancing back from the giant. She kept swinging the hatchet, driving his hand away as he tried to get a hold of her. Scott threw the final stone. It zipped past Amber to strike the man between his eyes. He blinked twice, his frame swaying for a moment, and then he fell back with a thunk. Amber spat on the ground and turned to find both women huddled together.

A shot rang out, the bullet ricocheting off the stone wall of the falls. Scott slid to a stop and scooped the older woman up, cradling her to his chest. He glanced at Amber, relieved to see her dragging the younger woman to her feet. He began to run. Another shot rang out, and he prayed they made it to the bend in time. Amber and the girl caught up in a flash.

They rushed past the curve, and Scott peeked back. No one was following, but he didn't know how long that would last. Amber stopped to grab her pack and slung it over her shoulders.

"We have a campsite just over there," the woman in his arms mumbled.

She shifted, and he realized his arm pressed against her bare skin. "Oh, Jeez. Amber, help." He set the woman down to lean against his girlfriend. He stripped off his shirt and helped pull it over her head. It hung past her knees, and he lifted her once more.

"We need to go," Amber said.

"I know the way," the girl said, her voice thick with emotion. "My name is Harper. That's my mom, Terri. I don't know how to thank you."

"Amber. That's Scott. You can thank us when we get away from those scumbags," Amber said, motioning for Harper to lead the way.

Scott followed, holding Terri's trembling form tight to his chest. She pressed her face to his shoulder and began to sob. They picked up their speed, and soon they were on an unfamiliar path heading away from the main trails.

CHAPTER NINETEEN

Billy sat with his back against the log. He pressed his palm against the side of his head and wondered if it would ever stop hurting. *That motherfucker has an arm.* Lenny rolled around, but the other two remained still. He contemplated leaving them behind and looking for a crew that didn't always think with their dicks. *Already scraping the bottom of the barrel with these morons.* He shook his head, wincing at the pain. In the end, they were likely the best he was gonna find. *Guess I'm stuck with them.*

He stood up and stepped over to Lenny, who no longer rolled around but lay still on his back. His eyes were open wide, and Billy glanced up to see what he was looking at. It was nothing but leaves and a patch of the sky.

"You gonna live?" he asked, holding his hand out.

For a moment, Lenny didn't react, but then he reached up and let Billy help him to his feet. With an exaggerated sigh, he stumbled over to Mike. Billy wandered toward Tristan and pulled up with a grimace. The man lay on his side with his dick resting on a mound of dirt. Ants crawled over his skin before disappearing into his pubic hair.

Tristan's eyes shot open, and he issued a wordless yowl. He rolled away, slapping at his crotch. Billy looked around, his eyes falling on the woman's discarded panties. He scooped them up and tossed them to Tristan. "Use these, dummy," he hissed at the man, cringing every time Tristan struck himself in the privates.

Tristan snatched the panties from the air and began to rub the ants from his skin. He struggled to his feet and sprang towards the falls. His shorts slid around his ankles and tripped him. He landed with a grunt on the hard ground and began to crawl forward, dragging his body into a shallow pool. He lay there moaning.

Mike sat straight, his gaze a bit unfocused and his arm clutched tight to his chest. He turned his attention to Lenny and blinked. "What the fuck happened?"

"Some babe broke your arm, and then her asshole boyfriend threw a fastball with this," Billy said, bending over to scoop up the blood-splattered, round rock. He bounced it in his hand and pointed to the side of his own head. "We're lucky the motherfucker didn't kill us."

Billy stepped to the sacks left behind and dug out some water bottles and a few granola bars. He handed them to Lenny. "You guys stay here, rest up, and wait for my return. We don't have time to fuck around. I'm going back to the truck to get the shotgun and the first-aid kit. Then we'll hunt those cunts down."

Billy walked away, moving as fast as his headache would allow. *More goddamn time wasted.*

★★★

"It's just up ahead," Harper said, glancing back at her mother, still held tight in Scott's arms. She had stopped crying, but her face remained buried against his bare skin.

Amber reached over and patted her shoulder. "He's got her."

Harper wanted to offer a reassuring smile but could only manage a grimace. After years of being out in the woods alone, they had never experienced anything remotely like what just happened. She swallowed, the image of the men looming over her flashing through her head. She could only imagine what her mother was thinking about.

"Thank God you showed up when you did," she whispered, her voice thick with emotion.

"Yeah, dumb luck, since we weren't even planning on coming to these trails. Once we get to your campsite, we'll need to call the cops and then figure out the next step."

Harper nodded. "Yeah, we're staying on some land my mom's friend owns." She pulled up, looking left, then right before pointing at a small opening between two large oaks. "Through there, I think."

"Yeah," Terri said. "That's it. Follow the trail for half a mile, then go right at the fork. You can put me down."

"I'm fine," Scott said. "Unless you're uncomfortable."

She shook her head and laid it back down on his shoulder. Harper led the way, and Amber fell in behind Scott. They walked in silence, following Terri's direction until they found themselves approaching the campsite.

"Jesus Christ," Harper hollered, running ahead.

"Wait," Amber called out, sharing a look with Scott as she rushed by.

Terri squirmed in his arms, and he set her down. She stumbled on her first step, held out her hand to stop Scott from helping her, and, after a deep breath, marched after the others. Scott followed close behind, waiting to reach out if she needed it. Standing next to the fire pit, Harper threw her hands up.

"What happened? Do you think those assholes found this first?" she asked, her voice cracking from frustration.

The tent was ripped to shreds and stuffed into the firepit. The log lay across the crumpled hood of the Outback. The front tires were flat, and after closer inspection, Scott discovered two large gashes in both.

"Hey, I've got a signal," Amber said with a fist pump. "I'll call the cops, and we can get some help out here."

Harper and Terri walked to the back of the vehicle. *At least there's no damage here,* Harper thought, and pulled out the keys to press the hatch button. It opened with a beep, and soon Terri was in fresh clothes from her main pack. She folded Scott's shirt up, and Harper grabbed some water bottles from the cooler.

"Anyone thirsty?" she called out as they reappeared from behind the vehicle.

Terri held out Scott's shirt. "Thank you."

He took it with a nod and pulled it over his head. Harper tossed him a water bottle, and he took a long drink, finishing half before taking a breath. Amber stepped closer and held out the phone.

"Can you tell them where we are?"

Terri took the phone, stepping away to answer the dispatcher's questions. A wave of exhaustion crashed over Harper, and she tumbled to the ground, her bottle slipping from her fingers. Amber and Scott leaned over her, and she wondered how long they had been a couple. She made a mental note to ask, right after she rested her eyes a bit.

CHAPTER TWENTY

Billy loaded his shotgun and stuffed extra shells into his pockets. He grabbed a water bottle from the cooler in the bed of his truck and drank it all in a few large gulps. He pulled his shirt up, wiping his face with the damp material. He was dripping with sweat and wanted nothing more than to slide into the truck, turn on the air conditioning, and leave. *Can this day get any worse?* His phone rang, and he slipped it from his pocket. The caller ID read Barney. *Now what?*

"Yello," he said, tapping the speakerphone icon. He placed the phone on the truck's hood and fished out the first-aid kit. He opened it but found only a couple of Band-aids and a pair of scissors.

"Just what the fuck are you idiots doing at Tioga Falls?"

Billy straightened up. *How the hell does he know where we are?* "Umm ..."

"Don't even think about bullshitting me, asshole," the man barked. "We just got a call that a bunch of meatheads attacked two women out there. They described Lenny and Mike to a fucking T. You're supposed to be getting ready to cook, not raping random hikers. Jesus H. Christ, what is going on in that pea-sized head of yours?"

"Well, shit, you know how those boys are," Billy said after a moment of silence. "Listen, it's under control. We'll take care of those hikers, and everything will be back on track."

"The hell you will. I'm on my way to them right now, and I'll take care of it. They're camping on the Day's property, and they're expecting someone from the sheriff's office. You shitheads are just lucky I took the call."

"Fine," Billy said, snatching up the kit and shotgun. He began to walk back. Bursts of static interrupted the call.

"Goddamn right, it—"

The call dropped, and Billy slipped the phone into his pocket. He started to jog. Nothing had gone the way he thought it would today, but he was sure of one thing. He wasn't about to let that "Barney Fife" mother fucker take care of anything.

CHAPTER TWENTY-ONE

"She's waking up," Terri called out in relief.

She sat on the ground, her daughter's head resting in her lap. Scott and Amber looked up and offered smiles. They sat on the log, now on the ground in front of the Outback. Terri thought they should leave it be but didn't say anything when they moved it. *Not like they're gonna dust it for prints.* The rest they left the same.

The sun dipped lower, and Terri wondered if they shouldn't clear out the firepit and get it ready in case the police didn't show up until after it got dark. *Who knows how long it might take to send someone out here?* She glanced up to find Scott standing closer and holding out a water bottle.

Harper shot up, barely missing the bottle, and issued a wordless cry. She blinked in confusion, shying away from Scott as he towered over the two women.

"Shh," Terri said, stroking her daughter's hair. "It's okay."

Scott motioned with the bottle, and after a moment's hesitation, Harper took it. She drank a bit before offering it to her mother.

"I hope they get here soon," Amber said.

Terri nodded her agreement and took a long drink from the bottle. She opened her mouth to suggest making the fire when a siren squawked. Scott turned and waved before stepping to the back of the vehicle. All three women joined him as the police cruiser slowed to a stop.

A man in uniform stepped out, looking exactly how Terri imagined a small-town sheriff would. He was tall, and while he carried a few extra pounds, she thought he seemed to be in decent shape. He wore dark aviator glasses and had a thick, brown mustache. He stared at them for a moment and then, after a nod, stepped forward.

"Hello, folks, my name is Deputy Lyman. Am I safe to assume y'all are the ones who called in the attack?"

"Yes, sir," Terri said. She stayed next to Scott and Amber. Harper hovered behind the three. "Four men attacked us … my daughter and I."

She expected her voice to catch when she said it out loud, but instead, a hot rage ignited in her belly. *Our last vacation ruined by a bunch of ... of ... monsters.* Harper placed a hand on her shoulder and squeezed.

"And vandalized her car," Scott said, his finger pointing to the front of the vehicle.

"Huh. So, you think those boys did this as well?" he asked as he moved closer to investigate the car. He studied the damage done to the wheels and the hood of the vehicle. "Was the log up here?"

"Yes, sir," Scott said, stepping over to the deputy. "I thought it would be okay to move it so we could sit. Sorry."

"Was it easy?"

"What?"

"To move it?" the deputy asked with a huff. Scott shook his head, and the man turned his attention back to the car. Terri leaned closer to hear his mumbles. "What the hell was Billy thinking, letting Mike and Lenny loose?"

Terri grew still. *How does he know their names?* She wrapped her arms around Harper and stepped back.

Scott glanced at them before returning his attention back to the deputy. "What's the next step? Paramedics? More deputies?"

"Oh, there won't be any paramedics," the deputy said, flashing a quick smile that was anything but reassuring. "Too difficult to navigate out here. I'll take 'em to the hospital. Just wanted to see the scene and get a better idea of the situation."

"Okay," Scott said. He straightened, his eyes locked on the man. "How about you take us to my car, so we can follow y'all to the hospital."

The deputy walked back to his cruiser, striding past them as if they weren't there. He stopped at the back and popped the trunk with his key fob. He disappeared for a moment, and Terri motioned for everyone to move close.

"I never said their names," she whispered. "On the phone, I just described them but not the names they used. I swear he just mumbled two of them."

The slamming of the trunk brought their attention back to the deputy's vehicle. Terri's stomach twisted in a knot at the sound of a shotgun being pumped.

"The last thing I need is a bunch of unwanted attention back here. I'm not saying they weren't wrong to hassle y'all, but boys will be boys."

Terri shuddered and fought back tears when Harper began to sob. Scott shuffled backward, forcing them behind the Outback. Amber tried to surge past him, but he blocked her with his arm.

"Don't," he hissed. "This is our only shot. You need to help them make it to the woods. I'll meet y'all at the fork, and then we head back to our car."

"He's gonna kill us," Terri said, her head in a fog.

"Not if I can help it. So grab whatever you need as long as it won't slow y'all down."

Scott motioned for them to duck down behind the vehicle. Lyman advanced with his shotgun aimed toward them. Scott slid to the corner and squatted. Terri slipped a cinch sack over Harper's shoulders. The deputy stopped a few feet away.

"Feels like a case of wrong place, wrong time for you good people," he said with a chuckle.

"What the fuck is going on?" Harper asked, her voice high and filled with confusion.

"Probably for the best if you don't ask any more questions," Lyman answered.

"Dude is covering up for those assholes we met back at the Falls ... right?" Scott asked while he searched the ground for more rocks.

"Not so much covering their asses as protecting my investment," the deputy replied. "And this way, you can be sure no one will interfere with y'all's bodies ... probably."

"Fuck off," Amber barked, crouching down to slide behind the front of the vehicle.

"Y'all need to understand this is over," Lyman called out. "I promise if you make me run, this is gonna get messy."

Scott patted the grass around him, his eyes locked on the shotgun. Amber reached into her pack and pulled out a folding knife and a flashlight. Terri snatched the flashlight and motioned for her daughter to take the weapon. Then she helped Amber slip on her pack.

"Won't that be too heavy?"

"For a mere mortal perhaps," Scott said, the lightness in his tone downplaying the seriousness of the situation. "Stick with Amber. She'll keep you safe."

"Babe?"

Scott locked eyes with Amber and winked. "Just get them to the fork. Love you."

He stood and flung a rock toward Deputy Lyman, striking him on the shoulder. The man jerked back, forcing the barrel towards the sky. The shotgun roared, and Scott pulled back to throw another rock. Terri grabbed Harper's hand, and the two rushed after Amber. She was already a few feet ahead of them and pulling away.

Lyman barked out a string of curse words, and the shotgun fired again. Terri glanced over her shoulder, surprised to see the deputy on his back and the shotgun lying a few feet from his grip. Scott was running towards the trees to the right of them. *We're going to make it.* A grin split her face, and she turned her head forward. Amber stopped a few feet from the trees and motioned them to hurry. Her eyes followed Scott as he ran in the opposite direction.

"Hurry, before that fucker gets back up. We're almost there," she cried out.

Terri's grip tightened on her daughter's hand at hearing the echo of her thoughts. Her mouth opened, but the words froze on her tongue. A shotgun roared once more, and Amber's head disappeared into a fine red mist. Harper's scream was lost in the low hum building in Terri's ears.

Amber's body swayed for a moment before the weight of her pack pulled it to the ground.

The man from the log stepped out from the tree line with a broad grin and raised his shotgun. Just behind him were the others. Terri's heart dropped. *Please, God, no.* She jerked at Harper's arm, pulling her more to the right. The low hum drowned out all the noise, but she was sure she was screaming. Her heart pounded against her chest, and she struggled to catch her breath. *We have to hide.*

They darted between the trees, and Terri increased their pace, tugging on her daughter's arm to keep up. Another blast sounded, and pellets shredded the foliage around them. She stumbled and gritted her teeth as the pain of multiple stings bloomed on her left arm and shoulder. They pushed deeper into the woods, and soon the hum died down. She slowed, glanced around, and sighed in relief when she saw no one was following.

"Momma ... they killed her," Harper whispered, her eyes wide and unblinking. "They killed her and we're next. Oh lord, we're next, Momma."

Terri hugged her daughter, unable to remember the last time Harper had called her anything but Mom. "No, baby. We still got a chance. Just be strong, and we'll get away. You'll see."

CHAPTER TWENTY-TWO

"What the fuck was that?" Deputy Lyman hollered. He struggled to his feet and dusted off the seat of his pants, his shotgun pointed to the ground. "I told y'all I would take care of them."

"Seems pretty hard to take care of much of anything lying on your back," Mike said through gritted teeth.

"Mike has a point," Billy said, offering a lopsided grin. "Plus, you have no idea the amount of trouble I've saved us by killing that bitch. She's a Goddamn Chuck Norris with tits."

Lenny pointed to his groin and nodded his agreement. He squatted by the body and jerked her shorts and panties down to her calves, then slapped her ass and stood.

"Now listen here," the deputy said, the color draining from his face. "There will be no interfering with that body while I'm here."

Billy released a belly laugh and threw his arm around Lyman's shoulder. "Jesus Christ, of course not. He's just setting up the scene ... same as you planned, I figure. Now, while he does his thing, we need to help the other boys. What kind of first-aid kit do you have?"

"Just a standard over-the-counter one. Why?"

Mike held up his arm. Tristan simply stared off, rocking back and forth quietly. His face was beet red, and he chewed on his bottom lip. They walked back to the cruiser, and Lyman leaned the shotgun against the bumper. He removed the kit, and Billy grabbed a recent issue of *Sports Illustrated*.

Billy motioned for Mike to hold out his arm. He folded the magazine around the break and wrapped it with tape from the kit. He dug out some sting relief packs and tossed them to Tristan. "Go take care of those bites. You must be going crazy."

Tristan tore open the first one and jammed the wipe down the front of his pants. He dropped it to the ground and tore open another. When he finished, he issued a sigh and put the rest in his pocket.

Mike leaned against the side of the cruiser; his breathing heavy. Billy held up a packet of acetaminophen. "You got anything stronger for Mike's pain?"

Deputy Lyman sighed and leaned back into the trunk. "Yeah. I always keep a few Oxy around in case we need to make a stronger case."

Billy locked eyes with Mike and nodded towards the trunk. They grabbed both ends and slammed it down on Lyman's head. A loud crunch sounded, and Billy motioned again. With the second blow, the deputy's legs went limp, and they let the trunk go. His hat lay off to the side, and blood ran from a deep gash on the back of the man's head.

Billy reached in and grabbed the bag of pills. He tossed them to Mike. "Go easy on 'em."

Mike popped two into his mouth and crunched down. He held out the bag, but Tristan shook his head, his hand absentmindedly scratching at his crotch. Billy pulled the deputy's handcuffs and revolver from his belt and tucked them into his waistband. He grabbed a pair of walkie-talkies and checked to see if they worked before handing one to Mike. The other he slipped onto his belt.

"Lenny's had plenty of time to see if his dick works," Billy said, tossing a box of shotgun shells to Tristan. "Time for him to load this box and anything else he wants into one of those cinch sacks. Mike, help me get this lump of shit into the front seat."

They dragged the deputy from the trunk and stuffed him into the driver's side of his cruiser. A low moan slipped past his lips, and Billy handcuffed him to the steering wheel. Lenny walked up, an odd smile on his face and his zipper down. In his right hand, he held one of the sacks, and in his left, a small gas can.

"Mike, get the deputy's shotgun."

Billy motioned for Lenny to hand him the can and began to dump the amber liquid on the deputy and the inside of his car. Lyman awoke with a sputter. "What the fuck?"

"I think this partnership is at an end," Billy said around the cigarette clenched between his lips. He took a deep drag and let the smoke blow out his nose, then flicked it into the cruiser. Lenny clapped his hands and danced around when a loud whoosh sounded. The deputy screeched, and Billy kicked the driver's side door closed. "See you in hell."

CHAPTER TWENTY-THREE

Scott slowed to a walk, his mind reeling. Memories ran through his head: meeting Amber, their first kiss, the first time they made love, and how his heart pounded when he bought the engagement ring. The memory shifted to him glancing over and seeing her head disappear into a cloud of red mist. He hunched over, vomit spewing onto the ground. The love of his life gone in the blink of an eye.

His stomach heaved again, but there wasn't anything left. He wiped the back of his hand across his lips and straightened. *Now what?* Scott glanced around, freezing when the sound of rustling leaves came from his left. His hands balled into fists. *I won't go down without a fight.*

Scott's breath caught when Terri and Harper stumbled from the foliage. He rushed over to the women and wrapped his arms around them, muffling a surprised squeak from

Harper as her face pressed against his chest. Once they realized it was him, they relaxed enough to return the hug.

Terri pulled back, looked up, and offered Scott a sad smile. "I am so sorry ..."

He shook his head, cutting off her words. "I can't think about that now. We need to get moving before those animals find us. We have to assume the sheriff is in on this since his deputy was ... Whatever this is." He knew if he lingered on Amber, he wouldn't be any use to the women. They still needed him.

Harper slipped the sack off her shoulder. "I think there's some water in here."

Scott took it and dug around. "Even better, we have some protein bars and a lighter." He took out the water bottle, unscrewed the cap, and rinsed out his mouth before taking a long drink.

A shotgun fired off in the distance, then a voice called out. "Listen up, dickhead. You're not getting past us, so if you're with those bitches, send 'em out, or things are gonna get nasty."

"You can't do that," Terri blurted out.

Scott nodded. "It's okay; that's not going to happen. We'll go this way a bit and then double back. This way we can circle around the Falls. Should only take an hour."

"It will be dark soon," Harper said with a quiver.

"Your mom has a flashlight, and you've got a lighter; we'll be okay."

Scott took one more drink, slipped the bottle back into the sack, and handed it to Harper. He started to walk, following a naturally made path. He needed to get these women to safety. Then he'd figure out a way to make those rednecks pay.

Billy waited at the edge of the trees, the shotgun resting on his hip. With each man armed, he felt they should be able to finish this pretty quick. *Then we can finally find the fucking weed.* He smiled at the thought, aware that he no longer needed to cut in the deputy. Killing the man was a risk, but after they finished off the boy scout and those bitches, it would be easy enough to make him the fall guy.

"Well, boys," he called over his shoulder. "Looks like they're not taking the offer. Mike and Lenny, y'all go the way

Ace ran. Tristan and me will head in the direction of those bitches."

"But—"

Billy held up his hand to cut Mike off. "Don't you worry none. The plan is to bring him back to finish up our little scene, and those ladies are going to put in overtime to pay back for today's little mishap."

Lenny nodded, punched Mike in the arm, and waved the deputy's shotgun over his head. They darted into the woods. Billy turned his attention to Tristan and studied him a moment in silence. *He's not looking so good.* His eyes were bloodshot, and he kept scratching at his crotch. The side of his forehead was swollen, and a dark bruise was already forming around the lump.

"You gonna be okay?'

Tristian offered a nod. "Right as rain, now let's find those bitches."

Billy motioned to the spot the women entered the woods. "That's the spirit."

CHAPTER TWENTY-FOUR

"Man, did you see how her head just disappeared?" Mike asked for the tenth time.

He popped another pill in his mouth and crunched down. His eyes glazed over, and a soft hum sounded from his throat. "Too bad we'll never know just how sweet that pussy was, huh?" He glanced at Lenny and nudged him with his elbow. He winced at the sudden movement, but the pain itself was nothing more than an afterthought. Lenny shrugged and offered a sly smile. *Sometimes, I wish this fucker could speak.*

They stomped through the woods, unconcerned with the noise they made. Lenny held the shotgun against his shoulder, but they'd been hunting enough that Mike knew how quick he could be ready. If they were lucky, they'd stumble onto that rock-thrower bastard before he realized they were there. A sharp jab of pain in his forehead brought tears to his eyes. *Don't think I could take another one of those fastballs.*

God willing, they'd shoot that prick in the gut and drag his ass back to the campsite. Let him die nice and slow staring at Lenny's spunk oozin' out of his girl's snatch. He barked a quick laugh, which sent another jolt of pain through his head. *Gonna make Ace suffer for sure.*

"So, I'm thinking now that the law's out of the way ... Billy's connections aren't really all that important," Mike said with a sly smile of his own. He watched Lenny from the corner of his eye. The little man continued to walk as if he didn't hear Mike's statement, but after a few feet, he nodded his agreement. "Great, so now all we got to do is find the weed and Billy's setup. Then we'll be large and in charge. The only other question will be if T-dog wants to get on board."

Lenny swung the shotgun and held it like he was aiming at the man. He pulled it back, imitating it being fired, and shrugged.

"Damn straight," Mike said. "He's either with us or against us, but we'll let him decide."

Scott crouched behind some bushes as Mike and Lenny strolled by. They didn't seem concerned with the noise they were making, and he wondered where the rest of their gang was. Depending on how spread out they were, it would make it that much harder for Scott to double back with the women. *Goddamn it!* He closed his eyes in frustration and bit down on the inside of his mouth until he tasted blood.

His eyes popped open. *Did he say the deputy was dead?* Scott leaned forward, straining to pick up the rest of their conversation as they pulled away. The shorter man stopped and mimed shooting something with the shotgun. Scott took a deep breath and fought the urge to rush them. *I have to get Terri and her daughter to safety.* He grabbed on to the thought, knowing it was what Amber would have wanted.

The men disappeared, and Scott counted silently in his head. At fifty, he stood and hurried off towards another cluster of bushes. He slipped through them, ignoring the branches scratching at his skin, and found Terri gently rocking her daughter. He squatted down and pointed to the northwest. "Two just walked by, and it sounds like they also killed the deputy."

Terri nodded, but Harper stared blankly ahead. Her mother stroked her hair in rhythm with the rocking. Tears leaked from the girl's eyes, but she made no move to wipe them from her cheeks. Scott glanced over his shoulder, peering through the leaves to make sure no one was there. He clapped his hands in Harper's face, his fingertips narrowly missing her nose.

She flinched back and began to blink. "What—"

Scott held up his hand to cut her off. "There's no time for this. If you want to make it out of these woods alive, you need to pull yourself together. Once we get to my car, you have my permission to lose your shit. Until then, I need you focused."

Harper weakly nodded. Terri glared at him while he spoke but stayed quiet. Harper wiped at her cheeks and released a shuddered breath.

"You're right ... sorry," she said in a shaky whisper.

"We're facing at least two groups, maybe three if I misheard about the deputy. I'm not sure the best idea is doubling back but going the opposite way. Maybe we can find a house or a spot where our cells have reception," Scott said, pointing behind the women.

Terri nodded. "Yeah, my friend's parents live near here. We had okay reception over by the site, but only by the car."

Harper pulled out her phone and checked. "Zero bars."

Terri checked her phone and shook her head. "Same."

"Let's get moving, and y'all keep checking for bars," he said.

He stood and held out his hands, helping each woman to her feet. He glanced back one last time before motioning for them to follow.

CHAPTER TWENTY-FIVE

Billy glanced up and frowned at the sun sinking down. *Need to wrap this up.* He didn't want to be looking for those fuckers in the dark. Tristan passed him, staring straight ahead and shuffling through the undergrowth. He scratched at his crotch and let out a groan. His foot caught on a root, and he stumbled forward before regaining his balance.

Billy shifted the shotgun off his shoulder. *Might be best to put him out of his misery.* A burst of static came from the walkie-talkie at his belt, followed by Mike's voice.

"Think we got a bead on where they're headed, boss."

Billy grabbed it and clicked the button to speak. "And where is that?"

"Southeast. They go far enough, they'll hit houses."

"Shit." Billy paused a moment to spit off to the side. The last thing they needed were more witnesses. "Well, y'all need to make sure that doesn't happen. We'll start heading in that direction to cut them off."

He clipped the walkie-talkie back on his belt and called out to Tristan. For a moment, there was no answer, then a wordless cry sounded off in the distance. He rushed forward, pushing through the foliage until popping out at the top of a sloping hill.

Tristan spun around and motioned toward the rows of plants dotting the hillside. "We found Jay's weed."

★★★

"Can we just take a break?" Terri asked between gasps. She leaned her hand against a tree and hunched over. Harper hovered nearby, unsure what to do.

Scott glanced back and stopped. "Yeah, I guess so." He pointed towards the top of a rise. "I'm going to head up there and see if I can find these assholes. If we're lucky, they're still heading in the wrong direction."

She kept her eyes on the ground but offered a weak nod. "Can you get me some water, hon?"

Harper dug into the sack and pulled out a water bottle. She unscrewed the cap and held it out with a shaky hand. "Here, Mom."

Terri straightened, grabbed the water, and took a long drink. She wiped the back of her hand across her mouth and handed the bottle back. "You need to drink some also."

Harper hesitated but, after a moment, drank the rest. She dropped the empty bottle and cap back in the bag. "We're not gonna make it home, are we?" she asked, her voice cracking.

Terri stepped closer, pressing her palm against her daughter's cheek. "Don't you dare think that. We're getting out of here."

Harper leaned into her mother's touch, and a single tear slipped from her eye. Terri wiped it away with her thumb.

"We have to go," Scott said, suddenly behind them. He grabbed Terri's elbow and pulled her back. "If I need to carry you, just say so, but they—"

Bark exploded from the tree next to them, and Harper's scream was lost in the echo of a shotgun blast. Scott flinched, turning his head as the scraps of wood peppered his face. Terri grabbed Harper's hand and jerked her into motion. They rushed past Scott, and another blast sounded.

"Run left," Scott hollered. "There's cover up there."

Terri ignored the burning in her calves and willed herself to go faster. Harper's fingers tightened their grip, driving her nails into her mother's skin.

"Woo-hee, look at them run," a voice called out from behind. "I don't think my dick could get any harder."

"Ignore them," Scott called out with a grunt. "They're just trying to fuck with your head."

Well, it's working, Terri thought, trying her hardest to ignore the images flashing in her head from earlier. She knew it was over if they got caught. Another blast echoed after them.

"Oh shi—," Scott cried out, the word drawn out before it cut off.

Terri glanced back, worried he'd been hit.

"What happened?" Harper asked, her voice frantic.

Terri could only shake her head and pull on her daughter's arm to keep her from stopping. Scott was gone, and they were on their own now.

INTERLUDE THREE

"What is that? Is anyone there? Oh God, it's on me ... get it off. Get it off. Get it offffffff!"

CHAPTER TWENTY-SIX

Billy spat off to the side. *What a waste of fucking time.* He frowned at the thought and glanced at Tristan. While he wanted nothing more than to kick Mike and his circus freak's asses, he got some pleasure imaging his fist crushing into this poser's face.

"What?" Tristan asked, looking up for the first time since they left the weed.

"I want to make sure we're on the same page. Don't let those two know we found the weed. Let's just get this taken care of so we can get back on track."

"Sure, you're the boss," Tristan said, offering a nod to punctuate the statement.

They continued in silence until a squawk came from the walkie-talkie at Billy's belt.

"It's a good-news-bad-news kinda situation," Mike said. "He disappeared, but we're gaining on the ladies."

"What the fuck do you mean disappeared?" Billy growled into the walkie-talkie.

"I mean he was running with them, and then he wasn't. If you want us to stop and go back, I'm sure we can figure it out."

Billy closed his eyes, crunching them tight as a dull ache began to grow in his forehead. "Not right now. Just get those two bitches. They owe us for all this trouble they caused."

"Ten-four," Mike said with a chuckle.

★★★

Scott woke with a groan. *Jesus, everything aches.* He ignored the thought and tried to blink away the starbursts before him. Light streamed down from above, and after staring at it for a moment, he realized he fell into a cave. Muffled voices came from overhead, and he pushed back into the shadows.

He strained to hear what was being said, but other than a burst of static, he couldn't make anything out. The voices faded, and Scott released the breath he'd been holding. He ran his hands over his body, searching for any injuries. He hovered over his knee, terrified to find it reinjured.

"Quit being a pussy," he grumbled before probing at the brace. His fingers slipped past the material, and he poked around, grateful to discover it was no worse than before. "Thank God, now if only I can do something to stop this pounding."

Scott pressed his palm against the side of his head, trying his hardest to ignore the steady throb in his temple. He struggled to his feet, using the wall to balance. He felt a rumble through the stone. *What's that?* When he couldn't come up with an answer, he moved forward.

The round cavern tapered into a tunnel. Scott paused at the edge, glancing back at the sunlight for a moment. *Maybe I can get back up?* He let the thought fade as his eyes darted around and confirmed there was no viable way up without help, then turned his attention back to the tunnel before him.

The tunnel plunged into darkness after a few feet. His chest tightened, and for a moment, he wanted nothing more than to run back and lay down under the light. Terri and Harper's faces flashed before him, and his cheeks grew hot.

They still need you. And that meant he needed to get out of the tunnels.

Scott shuffled ahead, his left hand running against the rough stone wall. The vibrations grew stronger, and soon he could hear the rumble of water flowing. Off in the distance, he swore he could see a flicker of illumination. It didn't seem like sunlight, more like a lightbulb. *Impossible*, he thought, trying to figure out how such a light would get there.

He pulled closer, speeding up as the darkness dissolved into a shadowy haze. "Well, I'll be damned," he murmured, staring at the string of lights hanging at the top of the tunnel wall. "I wonder who put you there."

Scott took a deep breath. *The better question might be why.* He ignored the sudden images flashing through his head, aware nothing good would come of his imagination running wild. He needed to find his way out of the caves, and he hoped following the lights would do just that.

CHAPTER TWENTY-SEVEN

Terri gasped for breath. She fought the urge to glance back, terrified of what she might see. Harper ran in front of her, her arm held back so she could hold her mother's hand. She knew her daughter could run faster but was grateful the girl didn't.

"Woo-hee," one of the men hollered from behind.

Her feet tangled up, and she tumbled to the ground, her hand pulling free from Harper's. She resisted the urge to just lay there and pushed up onto her hands and knees. After a few deep breaths, she worked up the nerve and glanced back with wide eyes. No one was there. *No one you can see.* She shuddered at the thought.

"Mom," Harper gasped, rushing back to help her up.

Terri kept her eyes on the foliage as her daughter helped pull her up. The branches began to shake, and the one named Lenny stepped from the green. He aimed the shotgun at them but didn't pull the trigger. She bolted, tugging her daughter's arm to follow.

"Run."

The two women ran a few feet before Terri zigged to the left, forcing Harper to follow her. They continued to run in a haphazard manner. The shotgun fired, the pellets shredding the trees and bushes to their left. They darted back to the right, and Terri ran faster. Her lungs ached, and she knew she couldn't keep this pace up for very much longer.

They burst from the trees into a clearing. Terri slid to a stop, and Harper crashed into her, taking them both down. Moaning, she leaned up and saw the two men walking towards them. The big one raised his hand and angled it to block the light from the setting sun. *They can't see us.*

She glanced around, squinting at a cluster of bushes across the clearing. "Over there ... hide," she whispered.

Harper nodded, her gaze locked on the two men as they approached. Neither seemed to have noticed them yet, and Terri prayed for their luck to continue. They scrambled through the clearing, staying as low as possible, and dove into the green undergrowth. Terri took a shuddered breath and checked the men again. They had stopped walking and were now arguing. The two men pointed in different directions, and while she couldn't hear the words the big one said, she could tell he was growing frustrated.

She motioned for Harper to move, and they crawled deeper into the undergrowth. Terri bit down on her lip to stifle the cry of joy rising from her chest. They were in front of a cave opening, camouflaged by the thick branches of the bushes and some vines hanging from above. She crawled into the darkness and turned to watch through the gaps in the foliage. Harper sat next to her and hugged her pack tight.

Terri leaned over and whispered into Harper's ear. "If we're lucky, they'll walk right by."

She watched them come closer, and Lenny pointed in the opposite direction. The big one shook his head. "I'm telling you this place seems familiar." Terri could hear the anger in each word, and she hoped Lenny was able to convince him he was wrong.

There was a radio squawk, and a voice sounded. "Hey, dipshits, we're here."

The big one stepped back into the trees, and with a huff, Lenny followed. Terri counted slowly to one hundred, and when no one returned, she whispered to Harper, "Let's go."

Terri clicked on the flashlight and crawled further back. The cave was oval in shape, with a large tunnel opening off to the left. She swung the light and, at the farthest end, saw a jagged slash of darkness. *What is that?*

Her light fell onto a scorch mark about halfway into the room. She stepped closer and noted the ash and partially burned logs. "Someone's been here, but it's been a while," she murmured, more to herself than to Harper, but the girl began to tremble at the words.

Terri pulled her close and pressed her lips on her daughter's forehead. The noise of footsteps crunching through the undergrowth filled the cavern, and the two women huddled down in silence. Terri clicked off her flashlight, and Harper buried her face in her mother's shoulder.

"So, you last saw 'em around here?" the voice from the walkie-talkie said. "The quicker we find 'em, the quicker y'all can have your fun."

Harper yelped into her mother's shirt.

"Did you hear that?" another man asked.

Terri watched with wide eyes as the man who'd tried to force himself on Harper came into view. Squinting, he studied the bushes. And though she wasn't sure if he could see them, her insides began to squirm. *Please, God ...*

"Holy shit," the man said, leaning back and looking towards the others. "There's an opening back here."

Terri's held breath came out in a hiss, and she stood, pulling Harper with her. "We can't stay here. If we get lucky, they'll think we went down that big tunnel."

They moved deeper into the shadows, and Terri locked her eyes on the spot with the mysterious darkness. She took small steps, worried one of them might trip if they moved too quickly. Outside the cave, the men's voices grew louder, but the words were unclear. She pressed her hand to the back wall and ran it over the stone towards the inky darkness she saw earlier.

She glanced back when the branches began to shake. Mike said with exasperation, "See, I told ya I recognized the area. That's the fuckin' Mouth."

Shit, shit, shit ... there's no time. Her throat tightened at the thought. Her hand slid over the rock and then pushed into a crevice. She turned, squirming into the opening, and moved a few steps before letting out a sigh.

She shuffled back and grabbed at Harper. "It opens up," she whispered, pulling her daughter into the slit.

They continued to move until the crack opened into a wider tunnel. The men's voices grew louder, but Terri slowed to a stop. She didn't want to go too far into the darkness until there was no other choice.

CHAPTER TWENTY-EIGHT

Billy watched Mike hack through the overgrowth to reveal the entrance. *Goddamn it, Simon ... it's brilliant.* A flash of annoyance ran through him at the thought.

"What's the Mouth?" Tristan asked, his hand still scratching at the front of his shorts.

"Back in the day, people came up here to party," Mike replied. The big man grew still, and his eyes glazed over. "Some chick said it looked like you were getting eaten by the hill when you went in. Plus, all the bones they found inside. What was her name?"

Billy thought a moment, then said, "Her name was something like Lisa ... no, Lesley."

"That's it," Mike said softly, clearing his throat before continuing. "Lesley Jones."

Lenny nodded and held his cupped hands in front of his chest.

"Yeah, chick had huge tits," Billy said, forcing a chuckle while shaking his head. "Shame what happened."

Tristan glanced around and, when no one elaborated, said, "Which was?"

Lenny tilted his head and ran his thumb across his neck. His tongue flopped out of his mouth, and he offered a grin.

"Yeah, she disappeared, and when they found her ..." Mike trailed off, his eyes locked on the opening.

"You mean when they found part of her," Billy said, stepping to the entrance.

Mike swallowed and nodded. "Yeah, her head was missing. And a leg, I think. Scared folks off, and they stopped coming out here."

"Which is exactly why Simon picked it." Billy stepped through the opening and motioned for them to follow. "Who has a light?"

Tristain fished out a flashlight and followed. "Someone has been here recently," Tristan said, shining the light across the floor.

"If I'm right, it was Jay or Pete," Billy said, motioning to Lenny to bring him the cinch sack.

He pulled out a flashlight and started walking around the room. Loud cracks came from the entrance, and Mike tossed in some of the branches before entering. Lenny piled them in the middle and lit them. Billy glanced at the fire, his attention quickly shifting to Mike, who shrugged.

"Looks like someone might have gone this way," Tristan called out from in front of the large tunnel to the left.

Billy ignored the man and kept walking around. He shined his light into the shadows the fire created in the cavern. "If y'all want to go check out the tunnel, fine by me. Just head back after a few minutes if you come up empty."

Lenny hopped over to the tunnel. Mike popped another pill into his mouth and pushed past the other two to enter the tunnel first. *Like he has something to prove*, Billy thought with a shake of his head. He swung his gaze back to the floor and stared at what looked to be fresh footprints in the dust. He kept his flashlight pointed down, hoping any residual light would be mistaken for firelight. He studied the scuffmarks, following them to the rock wall near the back.

Something strange about this wall. He frowned at the thought and leaned closer. His head tilted to the side, and he noticed a dark gash. It took him a moment to realize it was an opening. Just big enough for those women to crawl into. He shined the flashlight into the crevice and smiled.

"Well, hello, ladies."

★★★

"How's your dick, T-dog?" Mike asked over his shoulder.

"Don't worry about it," Tristan grumbled between scratches.

"Nothing some sweet pussy couldn't soothe, right?" Mike spun around with a wide grin on his face.

They came to a stop. Lenny offered a chuckle and slapped Tristan on the shoulder. He glanced at the two men, his eyes squinting in suspicion.

"What?"

"We're thinkin' it's time for a management change," Mike said, the smile still on his lips but his eyes suddenly hard. "You down?"

Tristan stopped scratching his dick and slid his hand to rest on his hip, inches away from the .38 special resting against his back. Mike slid closer, suddenly towering over him, and Lenny reminded him of an Organ Grinder's monkey as he hopped from foot to foot. He fought the urge to step back, knowing there wasn't enough space in the tunnel and, more importantly, how it would look to the others.

"You mean Billy?" he asked, impressed he was able to keep his voice so casual.

"Who the fuck else?" Mike asked with a huff. The big man glanced at Lenny and nodded his head toward Tristan with a get-a-load-of-this-guy expression plain on his face.

"Settle down, big fella," Tristan spat out. "What did y'all have in mind?"

"Accidents happen, but we need to make sure we find the goods before it does."

Tristan glanced down, mulling over his words before speaking. "Well ... you boys are in luck 'cause I know where the weed is growing."

Mike and Lenny shared a glance before Mike held out his fist for Tristan to bump. "Sounds like a hostile takeover is in our future."

CHAPTER TWENTY-NINE

Scott wrinkled his nose. *Jesus, what is that smell?* He took another few steps forward but stopped when the smell grew stronger. He wondered if he shouldn't turn back and retrace his steps.

"Is anyone there?"

Scott froze, unsure if he had really heard a voice. He strained to hear anything over the water's rumble. *Probably my imagin—*

"Please," a strained male voice called out. "Are you there?"

"Yes," Scott replied, turning in a circle to gauge where the voice was coming from. "Yes, I'm here. Where are you?"

"Oh my God," the man said with a sob. "I can't get free ... help."

Scott paused and leaned closer to discover a fissure in the rock wall hidden in the shadows. He held his hand out, surprised to feel waves of heat striking his hand. He stuck his arm into the opening, and after discovering it was only a few feet to the other side, he wiggled through. The stench was stronger on this side, and his eyes began to water.

Blinking back the tears, Scott examined the room. It was circular in shape, with a large wooden tripod in the center. A black cauldron hung a few feet above an open fire. Smoke drifted upward and disappeared through one of the many holes in the ceiling. He noticed a lot of refuse scattered haphazardly about the chamber. A thick iron spike was driven into the stone floor, securing a chain that ran across the room and ended attached to the ankle of a man lying on the floor.

"Holy shit … Are you okay?"

There was a low groan, but it was quickly lost in the crackle of the fire. Scott swallowed and started forward. A thick, dark liquid bubbled and churned in the cauldron, and a long wooden spoon hung from a nail driven into one of the legs of the tripod. With shaky fingers, he grabbed the utensil and held it just above the surface. With unblinking eyes, he stared as the tip of the spoon slipped into the soupy mess.

Scott began to stir. His breath caught when a piece of meat floated to the top. *Is that an ear?* Bile began to rise up his throat, but he continued to stir. It rolled away from him, dunking back beneath the churning surface to be replaced by a bobbing eyeball. Scott stumbled back, the spoon falling to the stone floor with a clatter. His gaze swung to the man, and he rushed to his side.

"Mister, we got to get out of here," he whispered, reaching out to shake the man's shoulder.

Scott froze. Something was wrong, and after a moment, he realized the man's clothes were on backwards. He leaned closer, noting the tears in the cloth, which revealed nasty gouges in the man's flesh. *Where's the blood?* He grabbed the man's shoulder and flipped him over, surprised how little he weighed.

A gasp slipped passed Scott's lips as he stared at the thick string stitched across the man's eyes and mouth.

"Oops," a child's voice said with a giggle. "You weren't supposed to look." The Goatman stepped out from the shadows and wagged his finger. "You're a naughty boy."

CHAPTER THIRTY

Mike wrinkled his nose. He'd killed enough animals to recognize the scent of death, but there was something else there, hidden underneath. He glanced at Tristan, but the man was oblivious. *That rock probably knocked the sense of smell out the fucker.* His jaw tightened at the thought of those two interlopers ruining all their fun. *At least that bitch is dead.* His lips curled into a smile at the thought.

Everything would be fine as soon as they got ahold of that momma bear and her cub. *A little pregame before the main slate.* He grew hard at the thought, and each step made his jeans rub against his hard-on. "We better find that trim soon," he mumbled, adjusting himself.

Tristan shrugged but stayed quiet. Sweat poured down his face, and Mike held out the bag of pills.

"Sure you don't want one?" he asked, shaking the bag.

Tristan shook his head. "I'd hate to deprive you."

"Suit yourself," Mike replied, slipping the baggie back into his pocket. "But you look like shit."

"Yeah, well, at least my heart's not going to stop," he snapped, his hand back to scratching at his groin. "Let's just figure this out."

"What's to figure out?" Mike said with a huff. "I'm pretty sure up ahead, the tunnel will split. After that, we'll find a hole. Lenny will bring back the boss man, and I'll tell him that you're hurt. With his attention on me, he won't be paying attention, and he'll take a tumble, and that's that."

"Pretty sure?" Tristan asked, his face still reflecting his doubt.

"Damn straight, T-dog," Mike replied, motioning with his good arm. "This ain't the first time me and Lenny have been in these caves. You'll see."

The two men continued in silence. Mike fought to keep the smile on his lips, but it melted away as the memory he'd ignored for so long rushed back.

It hadn't taken much convincing to get Becky to head out to the woods to meet them. A couple of pills and a six pack of Bud Light, and she was ready to party. Mike swiped at his forehead; Lenny made the fire too big, waggling his eyebrows when he said it would encourage her to strip down. And while he hadn't been wrong, the cave was a sauna now.

Lenny let out a grunt and shuddered. He climbed off Becky and stretched before pulling his jeans back up. He let out an exaggerated sigh and looked around for his shirt.

"Her snatch is still nice and juicy if you want one more go," he said, his voice a bit muffled by his t-shirt as it went over his head.

Mike shook his head. "Nah, I find it's more fun to stick it in 'em when they're breathin'."

He glanced down at the pretty girl's face, feeling nothing when he met the empty stare coming from those unblinking eyes. Little mouse thought she could fuck with the cats and nothing would happen. His gaze slid to her left hand, clenched in a fist, and he reached down to pry her fingers open.

"Dumb bitch shoulda realized you don't play when it comes to your stash," Lenny said with a chuckle. "I mean that pussy was good, but not that good."

Mike plucked the four pills from her palm and, after taking one, slipped the others back into a baggie. Wasn't the first time Mike ended up being rougher than he planned and wouldn't be the last. In the end, what did it matter? They'd drag her body a little deeper into the tunnels, and some wild animal would do the rest. When they got home, there'd be another one just like Becky waiting to make a trade.

Lenny reached down, grabbed her wrists, and began to drag her into the tunnel. Mike called out, telling him to wait a moment so he could take a piss, but Lenny didn't stop. He had that weird look in his eyes he always got around dead things, and Mike knew better than to press it. He fished his dick out and closed his eyes, barely listening to Lenny's non-stop chatter about the girl and her tits. His voice grew harder to hear the further Lenny got, and soon the sound of Mike's urine splashing against the stone wall drowned it out completely.

Mike jerked when Lenny's scream echoed down the tunnel. It was a wordless cry of agony that instantly cut short. He stuffed his dick back in his pants and jammed a branch into the flames. He strained to hear anything over the crackle of the fire. He rushed into the tunnel and called out for Lenny. There was no answer. Up ahead, he could see Becky's body lying on the floor, but Lenny was nowhere to be seen.

"Lenny, quit fucking around."

Mike stepped over the girl, and his breath caught. There was an opening in the stone floor. He guessed it was about four feet deep and almost the size of the tunnel, with just about a foot of room on either side to walk by. He squatted and held the torch out. Lenny lay at the bottom, a thick stake jabbed into his throat. Blood gushed from the wound, and Mike pulled off his shirt and dropped into the hole.

He let the torch fall to the ground and worked Lenny free as gently as he could. Blood gurgled from the wound, and he pressed his shirt against it. Lenny stared at him with shiny, wide eyes. His mouth opened and closed, but no words came out. Mike laid him on the floor of the tunnel and crawled out of the hole. He lifted his friend and froze when a voice spoke from the darkness ... his voice.

"I find it's more fun to stick it in 'em when they're breathin'."

That was the last time they were in the tunnels, the last time Lenny spoke a word, and the last time Mike had truly been frightened.

Tristan watched Mike from the corner of his eye. He couldn't quite place his finger on what exactly was the problem, but something was making the big man uneasy. He didn't think Mike was smart enough to know fear, and seeing it flash across his face sent a chill through Tristan. Before he could ask, Mike motioned to the split before them. The lights put up by Jay and Pete ran off to the right, but Mike pointed to the tunnel on the left.

"This is the one we want. Lenny will bring Billy here, and then we can take care of business."

Tristan nodded, and the men walked down the tunnel in silence. He watched Mike from the corner of his eye, but there was no way to see if the man's apprehension returned in the shadowy tunnel. He scratched his crotch. At this point, he just wanted to get all this over with and head to his doctor's office. After that, it would be a piece of cake manipulating these morons so he'd be top dog.

"There," Mike barked, the word pulling Tristan from his thoughts. The flashlight beam shined upon a discolored section of the stone floor. The big man's arm shot out and stopped Tristan in his tracks. He swung the light to their feet. "Look down."

Tristan glanced down and noticed the flashlight's beam reflecting off a thin bit of wire that ran across the tunnel. He squatted and studied it a bit.

Mike stepped over the wire and leaned over to pull up a dirty corner of a tarp. "These are all over the tunnels. Under here, we'll find a hole large enough for a man to fall into, and at the bottom, there are spikes. We didn't stick around to figure out who did it or why."

Tristan motioned for the big man to pull the tarp higher. He shined the light into the opening. "Huh, there *is* a hole there."

"No shit, Sherlock," Mike snapped. "I'm gonna scoot past it, and you're gonna head back to that crevice we saw by the entrance and hide. Once Billy boy passes, listen for the signal, and we're in business. If you don't hear it, then you know to take care of him when he heads back."

Tristan nodded, motioning for the man to hand over the shotgun. Mike hesitated, leaning close to study the man's face. They locked gazes, and after a moment, Tristan reached over and pinched his nipple.

"We don't have time for this nonsense," he said before twisting.

Mike slapped away the man's hand and chuckled. "All right … Jesus. I just wanted to make sure you're on the up and up with Lenny and me." He held out the shotgun.

Tristan grabbed it and shrugged. "There's too much at stake for me to turn back now."

"True dat," Mike said with a toothy grin.

CHAPTER THIRTY-ONE

Billy sucked in his stomach and tried to push into the opening—"God damn it,"—the words slipping out as he exhaled. He shined the light back in the tunnel, illuminating the backs of the women. He pulled his walkie-talkie out and hit the button. "Found 'em. Come on back."

"What? ... already ... way," Mike responded, bursts of static cutting off his words.

A hand landed on his back, and he jumped, dropping the walkie-talkie. "Jesus Christ!" he barked, spinning with his fists up. Lenny hopped back, a lopsided grin on his face. Billy dropped his hands and glowered at the man. "This never talking bullshit is getting old."

Lenny shrugged and motioned for him to follow him back to the chamber. Billy shook his head and pointed to the opening. "They're right in there. Go get them."

Lenny stepped closer, peering into the opening after Billy held up his flashlight. The women were almost out of reach of the light, and Billy wondered just how far the tunnel went. They darted to the left and disappeared.

"Listen, you go after them, and I'll go catch up with the others," Billy said, handing his flashlight to Lenny. "Maybe the two tunnels meet up. Take this just in case. You can make it beep to let us know when you have them." He pointed to the button on the walkie-talkie before clipping it to the man's belt.

Lenny turned sideways and slipped through the opening without any issue. The light bobbed up and down as Lenny scampered off. Billy turned and moved to the cavern. He double-checked his shotgun and the deputy's revolver. A flush of nervous energy ran through his body. *Lenny got here too quick ... Those assholes are up to something.*

He entered the larger tunnel and started to jog. He hoped it was his imagination, but he knew better than to ignore the feeling. A loud racket echoed through the tunnels. Billy pulled up, raising the shotgun to his shoulder. The noise reminded him of dropping empty beer cans from his balcony, and he wondered what was making the sound down here of all places. *Guess we'll see soon enough.*

Tristan hurried back to the split in the tunnel. He didn't want to bump into Billy on his way to the hiding spot. Wouldn't do to look like he was up to something. He bit his bottom lip. Truth be told, he just wanted to leave. His dick ached, and he wasn't sure if he was making it worse by delaying a trip to the doctor's. *Almost there*, he reminded himself. Hell, if it all worked out, those two apes would take each other out and he'd be the only one left standing. Well, Lenny was still alive, but he wasn't anyone to be worried about.

He stepped out into the lighted tunnel and released the breath he'd been holding for the last hundred steps. No one was there. He moved to the jagged fissure and stared at the opening. *Is there enough room?* He wasn't a fan of tight spaces, but he'd be fine if there was space for him to stretch out a bit.

Footsteps echoed down the tunnel, and Tristan squirmed out of sight. He tried to turn around but froze when Billy stomped by muttering to himself. He swallowed down the cry building in his chest, suddenly aware that there wasn't enough room for him to make the full turn. He either had to back out or push forward and hope it widened. The image of Billy's shotgun flashed into his head, and he wriggled ahead.

Once I turn around and face the exit, it will be okay, he told himself to keep from drowning in his rising panic. If he didn't hurry, he might miss the signal. He popped out into a slightly wider space and closed his eyes with a sigh. *Thank God.* He turned and strained to hear the signal. *Should have just shot the fucker when he passed.*

Doubt crept up from his belly, and he wondered why that hadn't been the plan. He held up the shotgun and, after a moment, checked, only to find it unloaded. His jaw clenched. *That motherfucking meth-head.*

A shotgun blast echoed through the tunnel, and he froze. *Oh shit, what if Billy caught on?* His mind raced, but he realized he only had one option. He needed to go check and, if Billy was still alive, deal with him like he always planned. He took a deep breath, hoping to steady his nerves, but gagged instead.

A heavy musk filled his nostrils and made his eyes water. He stepped back, trying to slide deeper into the crevice, but slammed to stop. He swallowed the lump forming in his throat, aware that whatever he was pressed against was both hairy and alive.

Tristan tilted his head back but saw only darkness. Strong hands wrapped around his arms, and a goat's head leaned into view. The light reflected off the empty black eyes, and salvia dripped from the creature's bottom lip onto Tristan's forehead. A scream built in his chest, but nothing came out save a high-pitched whimper.

"Don't be scared, little rabbit. I got you."

CHAPTER THIRTY-TWO

Scott woke with a start and sat up, slamming his head into the metal bars above. He grimaced as the pounding in his head fell in rhythm with the grumble of an unseen generator.

"What the fuck?" he mumbled, pressing against the knot growing on his forehead. He closed his eyes, and the image of the Goatman towering over him suddenly popped into his head. *Oh God* ... He swallowed and forced his eyes open. He glanced around, and while there was no sign of the Goatman, what he did see made his blood run cold.

The room was rectangular in shape, with tunnels at either end. Small fires burned throughout the room, but they created more shadows than light. Cages sat in three of the corners, and in the fourth, a makeshift drying rack stood with strips of pale hide hanging from the crossbars. Bones littered the floor, and a pyramid of skulls rested against the wall a few feet from the rack. Scott stopped counting at fifteen and turned his attention to the large table in the middle of the room.

Although his cage prevented him from seeing anything on the tabletop, he did see a hatchet buried into the corner of the dark brown wood. The sudden urge to pee pressed against his bladder, and he bit his bottom lip. *Have to get out.* His chest tightened at the thought, and he grabbed the bars before him. He guessed the bars were iron, though he couldn't be sure in the dim light. There was enough room to lie down flat but not enough to do much more than squat. He scrambled to the door at the end and found a thick, round lock.

"It's unlocked," a woman said from the shadows.

Scott jumped, issuing a high-pitched yelp before falling back on his ass. "Jesus, who's there?" he asked, instantly regretting the deep breaths he took to try and calm down his heart. "Wait … we aren't locked in?"

A woman leaned into the light and wrapped her grubby fingers around the bars. Dark streaks smeared across her face and clothes. Her hair hung in filthy clumps, and he realized there was no way to know what color it was until the poor woman washed off.

"It doesn't matter. We're already dead, just too fucking stupid to accept it," she said in a hollow voice.

"Bullshit, there's always hope …" Scott trailed off, the image of the Goatman once again flashing in his head. Laughter drifted from the tunnels, and the woman curled into a ball in the back corner of her cage. He fought the urge to follow her example, a chill running down his spine as the laughter seemed to grow closer. His head darted back and forth, unable to decide which tunnel it came from.

"Ah, ah, ah … someone has a potty mouth," a child said from the darkness.

Scott gasped as the Goatman stepped from the shadows, carrying a man over one shoulder. It slung the man onto the table and held him still with its left hand. The man struggled weakly and grabbed the wrist of the creature with his right hand. Scott watched with wide eyes, his lips moving in a silent prayer that the man might succeed in getting free, despite the fact he was one of their attackers. The Goatman reached over and retrieved a hatchet.

The beast shifted its weight and brought the hatchet to hover over its head. It turned its head towards Scott and offered a grotesque imitation of a smile. The man it held stopped struggling, his wide eyes now locked on the glint coming from the hatchet's bit. The Goatman brought the weapon down on the man's shoulder, driving the edge through cloth, skin, muscle, and bone. The man wailed, and Scott threw his hands over his ears.

"Who's hungry?" the Goatman said, his voice shifting to that of an older woman's. He held the arm up for a moment, shaking it so the man's hand offered an exaggerated wave. "Oh me ... me," it answered itself in the voice of a child before beginning to giggle.

Scott's stomach heaved as the little bubbles of a child's laughter filled his ears. The Goatman turned his attention back to the cage, and its eyes squinted in thought. A shudder ran though Scott, and he followed the woman's example, quickly curling into a ball. He flinched when the man's arm bounced off his cage's bars but didn't make another noise. He so wanted to close his eyes, but he couldn't tear his gaze from the blood gushing onto the floor. The man no longer screamed and instead made tiny mewing noises that turned Scott's bowels to water.

The Goatman leaned over, sniffing at the bloody stump. Its tongue snaked out, and it lapped at the blood dripping from the wound. A soft moan of approval came from the beast, and Scott's sphincter clenched. Tiny gasps came from the man, and he offered one final push to get free. The creature shook its head and smiled once again.

"Poor thing doesn't know it's over," the Goatman said, sounding identical to the woman in the cage.

Scott glanced her way, but she was still in a ball, her head covered. The hatchet rose once again, and when it came down, it cut through the man's neck. Vomit spewed out of Scott's mouth, splashing on the ground and through the cage's bars.

"Oh God," Scott moaned, his voice hoarse and shaky.

The Goatman grabbed the head and carried it to his cage. "Don't be scared, little rabbit," it said, switching back to a child's voice. It pressed the head between two bars until it stuck. "He'll keep an eye on you until I get back."

CHAPTER THIRTY-THREE

"Hurry," Terri said, her hand pressed against her daughter's back. She glanced back, and the flashlight beam temporarily blinded her.

She swung her head forward, blinking away the stars, and clicked her flashlight back on as the tunnel curved to the left. An exit appeared, and Harper sped up, pulling away from Terri's touch. She rushed through the opening, cried out, and disappeared from the flashlight's illumination as a loud clanking racket filled the tunnel.

"Harper," she cried out, fighting the urge to hurry after her.

Terri ran the light over the opening, shocked to find a thin wire stretched a few inches from the stone floor. She might have missed it, but the smear of blood across it caught her eye. She stepped over the wire and left the tunnel. A soft

176

green glow illuminated an immense cavern, showing her the gentle slope of the hill she stood on and where it ran into a wide, flat beach. Dark water lapped against the shore.

Terri swung the flashlight around, searching for her daughter. The beam landed on Harper's leg, a few feet from the bottom of the incline. She opened her mouth to call out, but her breath was driven from her lungs as the man chasing them slammed into her back. The flashlight flew from her hand, and she tumbled down the hill in the grasp of rough, clingy hands.

Terri slid to a stop with a grunt. She struggled to focus while the hands grabbed at her clothing. He pulled back hard on the collar of her t-shirt, cutting off her air as it pressed against her throat. She clawed at her shirt, her back bending until she thought her spine might break. Stars danced in her vision, and her fingers loosened before her arms slipped to her side. Terri managed a choked sob, then went limp.

He dropped her to the sand, and his hands ran down her back to stop just above her waist. He pushed her shirt up to expose her shorts, hooked his fingers into the waistband, and pulled both her shorts and panties down. She groaned when his hands returned, pressing against her ass and then sliding to her hips. She shuddered but was still too out of it to do much else.

Lenny rolled her onto her back, jamming his knee between her legs to force them to spread apart. His hands slipped under her shirt, creeping up her skin like spiders. Her insides turned to water, and she murmured for help. The words came out softer than a whisper, lost in the excited grunts he made when his hands roughly squeezed her breasts. He laid on her, his mouth hovering over her lips as he continued to fondle her.

His excitement grew and pressed against her. Terri's head flopped side to side, trying desperately to avoid his tongue. She winced when the slimy appendage slid across her cheek. A howl slipped past her lips, stealing the little bit of air she'd recovered. Her chest heaved, and he continued to squeeze her breasts.

Get up, Harper. Terri wasn't sure if she spoke the words or if they were just wishful thinking. She prayed her daughter heard them and escaped. Her body trembled, fear washing over her in rhythm to the waves lapping the shoreline. She closed her eyes and prayed she'd pass out, but her eyes bulged open when his fingers slipped inside her.

Harper woke to the sound of a wordless cry. Tears leaked from her eyes as pain seemingly crashed down on her.

She wrapped her arms around herself and tried to breathe past the agony. Her right ankle burned, and she could feel random aches and abrasions all over her arms and legs. A steady pounding settled behind her eyes, and her left ear felt like it was beginning to swell.

"Mom?" she finally managed to gasp. The only answer was the gentle splash of water striking the beach. She rolled onto her side and took a deep breath. A gentle green glow shimmered off the surface of a large lake, and after a moment, she struggled to sit up.

Down the shore, she could see the man who chased them in the tunnel thrusting into a shadowy figure. "Mom?" she asked, her voice straining against the tightness in her chest.

Harper struggled to her feet, took one step, and crumpled back to the sand when her right leg gave out. Her fingers dug into the sand, and she pulled herself forward, sliding to her knees so she could crawl towards them. She bit back a cry as each movement brought a jolt of pain through her body, forcing her to stop so she could collect herself.

After taking a deep breath, Harper lurched forward, and her hand came down on something hard. She wiped away the sand and found the heel of a man's boot. She recoiled and issued a sharp hiss of surprise. Leaning back, her gaze swept from the boot to the water, and she knew there was a partially buried dead man before her. A shimmer caught her attention as the soft green illumination reflected off something metallic.

Harper crawled closer and discovered a large screwdriver in the man's toolbelt. She grabbed it and found some comfort in the thick, heavy handle. She glanced up and saw Lenny's back begin to arch. He was less than twenty feet away, and she knew she was running out of time. *When he finishes, he's coming for me.* The thought echoed in her head until the blood pounding in her ears drowned it out.

Her mother cried out, and Harper scurried forward. The sand tore at her palms and ground into the cuts on her knees, but she ignored it all, her gaze locked onto the man's back as he began to shudder. She reached out and grabbed his hair with her free hand, tightening her grip until she felt it begin to tear from his scalp.

Harper shrieked and drove the tip of the rusty screwdriver blade into his back, pushing with all her might until the handle met his skin. She pulled it free and struck again. He swatted at her hand and tried to pull free, but she ignored him and slipped the screwdriver into his armpit. She jerked down on the handle, her eyes closing in satisfaction when his hot blood gushed over the handle and her hand. He went rigid, and his arms flailed about, but there was no direction to the movement. She pulled the shaft free once more and drove it into his neck.

Lenny quivered, and before he could do anything to stop the bleeding, he flopped forward. Terri issued a squawk as the man fell on her. Harper's eyes rolled up as a new wave of pain washed over her. She swayed for a moment and then slumped to the sand with a whimper.

CHAPTER THIRTY-FOUR

Billy stopped when Mike came into view. He shined his flashlight on the big man leaning against the tunnel wall. He never would have come this way if he hadn't heard the man calling for Tristan to hurry up.

"About time," he said, kicking off the wall and turning towards the light. "Oh, hey, bossman ... Thought you were T-Dawg."

"What do you mean?" Billy asked. "Why isn't he with you?"

Mike shrugged and clicked on his flashlight before answering. "Man said he had to shit. I've been waiting an eternity for him to get back here."

"And why didn't y'all head up the lighted tunnel?" Billy asked and scrunched his eyes in suspicion. Something was off, but he couldn't quite place his finger on it.

"We were going to, but there was a noise coming from this one, so we decided to check it out," Mike replied. He pulled out the bag of pills and popped one in his mouth.

Billy sighed. "How many of those have you had?"

Pretty sure I know what's off. He sighed again at the thought. *Should have limited the moron.* Mike shrugged and held up the bag. Billy clenched his jaw. *How is this idiot still standing?* He'd worry about it later. Now, he wanted to get everyone back to the main room so they could be ready when Lenny showed up with the women. It was time for them to blow off some steam and get their heads right.

"Call your boy on the radio ... see if he's done snatched the snatch."

Mike laughed and brought the walkie-talkie to his face. "Lenny, you got 'em?" He waited for a moment, but only static replied. He looked at Billy and shrugged.

"We think there's a shortcut up this way," Mike said, and pointed his flashlight's beam up the tunnel into the darkness. "We can make sure before Tristan gets back."

Billy watched the man step away. *Where's his shotgun?* He thought back and was pretty sure Lenny didn't have it when he showed up. *Why would he give it to Tristan?* The hairs on his neck and arm began to rise.

"Hey, wait a minute," he called out, hurrying to catch up and stop Mike from going too much further. The toe of his boot caught something, and he tumbled forward.

"Oh shit," he barked out, his left hand reaching out to soften the blow.

His foot came down on the dirty floor, and he cried out in surprise. The floor disappeared into the stone, and it took a second for his head to register it was a tarp. He continued to fall, everything seemingly running in slow motion. He pulled the trigger, and the shotgun roared. Mike howled and slipped from view. Billy twisted at the last moment to avoid a thick spear from jabbing into his face, only to have two more pierce his flesh. Pain overwhelmed him, and his world went black.

★★★

Mike sat up. The back of his leg and ass burned. He reached back and winced when he touched the damp holes in his jeans. *Fucker got me.* He hated removing buck shot, but he guessed it was better than the alternative. He crawled to the edge of the hole and smiled. Billy was caught on two spears, one in his side and the other poked through his forearm. *Serves you right.* He spat into the hole and stood.

"Fuckface is neutralized," he said into the walkie-talkie, a soft, steady hiss the only reply. "Goddamn it."

He inched around the edge of the trap, careful not to slip. He eyed the shotgun, his head moving side to side as he contemplated going for it. Billy shuddered and issued a low moan. Mike scampered to the other side, no longer interested in being around when the man woke up. *I'll just get mine back from Tristan.* He shuffled down the hall, wincing with every step.

Mike pressed his big hand flat against his butt cheek, happy to feel some relief with the pressure. He fished out the bag and snorted when he realized there was only one pill left. *Gonna need a refill.* He popped it into his mouth and quickly chewed it up, then wiped his brow with the back of his hand. A scream echoed down the tunnel, and he froze. Mike shivered. *Only heard a man scream like that once.*

Taking a deep breath, he forced himself to start moving again. The breath came out in a series of jagged coughs. *Kill for a beer.* A smile bloomed across his lips. *Guess I already have.* He stepped out of the dark tunnel, and a glint of metal on the floor ahead caught his eye. Whatever it was stuck out of the wall, and he squatted to get a closer look.

"Well fuck me," he said with a snort. He reached over and pulled his shotgun from the shadows.

Another scream echoed down the tunnel, and Mike straightened. He pressed the button on the walkie-talkie. "Lenny, it's time to roll. Meet me by the entrance, with or without those bitches."

He refused to glance back and started to walk back towards the Mouth. After a few steps, Mike pushed the pain away and started to run.

CHAPTER THIRTY-FIVE

Scott ignored the dead eyes watching him, grabbed the lock, and twisted the shackle away from the body. *Huh, she wasn't lying.* He pushed open the door and crawled out of the cage.

He couldn't help but glance at the tunnel the Goatman had disappeared into after the string of cans banged together. *Who else is down here?* He said a silent prayer it wasn't Terri and her daughter. He stepped over to the woman's cage and squatted. She studied him with empty, unblinking eyes.

"So, you ready to get out of there?" He removed the padlock and swung the door open.

She didn't move.

"Goddamn it!" he barked, and stretched his arm into the cage to offer his hand. "I'm not leaving you here. We need to go ... while it's distracted."

Sighing, the woman closed her eyes but reached out to take his hand. He helped her to her feet and, before he released his grip, shook her hand.

"I'm Scott and you are ...?"

"Not going to matter," she mumbled.

"Okay, can I call you Matter for short?" She stared at him until the silence became unbearable. He cleared his throat. "Sorry ... bad joke. It's been a ... day."

"Beth."

Scott nodded and stepped to the table. "We need some light, and, I'm thinking, this." He pulled free the machete he found wedged in the man's belt and held it out to her. "I'll let you decide which one you want."

She shook her head and wrapped some scraps of cloth around the end of a thick tree branch before jamming the end into one of the fires. She held up the torch and motioned towards the tunnel.

"Yeah, I was thinking the same thing. Let's go the opposite way."

They paused at the exit, and Scott stared into the darkness. Beth held the torch out, but its flickering light only went so far. He swallowed and took a step forward. The next step came easier, and he glanced back and forced a smile to his lips.

"Piece of cake. We'll be out of here in no time."

Beth shook her head and stayed still. He continued forward and disappeared into the darkness.

"Be a lot easier if I could see," he called out, trying his best to keep his voice even. Hurried footsteps were her only answer, and he released a shuddered breath when the torch's light caught up to him.

Billy woke with a groan. While he generally ached all over, the sharp, throbbing pain in his right arm concerned him. He shifted, crying out at the sudden agony radiating from his right hip. When his vision cleared, he noticed his flashlight was still on and shining against the wall. He reached out tentatively with his left hand, moving so slowly it reminded him of playing Operation back in the day. *Not sure I can take another buzz like that.*

"Come on," he said between clenched teeth, his fingertips a scant few inches away from the flashlight's butt.

He took a deep breath and leaned forward. His vision went red for a moment, then shifted white. He let loose a scream of agony, the wordless cry tearing at his throat until it was raw. He grabbed the flashlight and shifted back, struggling to remain conscious.

"God damn it. I don't have time for this," he said, spitting each word out like it were rotten. He was well aware he was making too much noise. The last thing he needed was one of those assholes coming back to finish him off.

Billy took a few deep breaths and then shined the light on his arm. An inch-thick wooden stake stuck through his forearm. He took another breath, this time smelling nothing but the sweet metallic tang of his blood, which dripped down to form a small dark pool. A wave of nausea washed over him, and he swallowed back the bile rushing up his throat.

He dropped the flashlight and grabbed his right arm at the wrist. *Now's not the time to be a pussy.* He jerked his arm up, using the left to help get him past the splintered point of the spike. His scream came out a strangled gurgle, and he pulled his arm to his chest. His eyes unfocused, and for a moment, he was sure he was going to pass out. Blood soaked into his shirt, and this time, he couldn't hold back the vomit when the hot coppery scent hit his nostrils.

You got this. He focused on those three words, repeating them over and over in his head. He pressed his palm to the cold stone and pushed, shifting up at his waist when he began to rise. His body trembled, and white-hot pain pulsed in his side. His injured arm buckled, and he slid back down, the wooden stake jabbing deeper into his flesh. He howled in agony, biting down on his bottom lip until he tasted blood, but refused to stop trying to rise. Billy pulled free from the spike and shifted so he could collapse onto the hard stone.

"Mother. Fucker," he growled at the pain pulsing through his arm and hip. His lips pulled back into a grimace, exposing his blood-soaked teeth as he snarled. "I'm going to kill those bastards."

CHAPTER THIRTY-SIX

"Oh, thank God," Terri said with a sob when Harper opened her eyes.

She wrapped her arms around the girl and pulled her to her chest. Harper stayed rigid for a moment before melting into her mother's embrace. Tears leaked from the corners of her closed eyes, and her breath caught on a whimper.

"It's gonna be okay," Terri whispered, stroking Harper's hair.

Harper tried to fight it, to act like it was no big deal, but in her head, all she saw was the screwdriver shaft sliding into the man's flesh. She buried her face into her mother's chest, desperate to stop the memory from replaying in her head over and over again, and began to bawl.

"That's it," Terri whispered. "Let it all out."

A squawk came from the body, and both women jumped.

"Fuckface is neutralized."

Harper pulled back, staring at her mother with wide, shiny eyes. Her hands felt sticky, and she looked down, suddenly aware that his blood covered her skin and clothes. A wail started deep in her chest, and she scrambled to the water's edge, dunking her hands beneath the surface. Her mother followed and gently placed her hand on Harper's back.

"Get it off," Harper screamed, scratching at her skin with her fingernails.

Another squawk sounded before the voice spoke again. "Lenny, it's time to roll. Meet me by the entrance, with or without those bitches."

Terri grabbed Harper's shoulders and pulled her away from the water. "We have to go. Now." She helped Harper up. "Can you walk?"

"I think so," she answered in a shaky voice, closing her eyes, not wanting to see she failed to clean all his blood from her skin. She took a hobbled step forward, then another, and, on the third, opened her eyes and nodded toward the hill. "I'm not sure I can get up there without help."

"Don't worry, baby," Terri said, wrapping her arm around Harper's waist. "I'm always here to help."

★★★

Terri motioned for Harper to stop. They were almost back to the cave, and she wanted to check first. She clicked off the flashlight and inched forward to the opening. A fire burned low in the middle of the room and looked like it might go out any minute. She stared into the shadows, squinting to see if she caught any movement. Biting her bottom lip, she slid back to her daughter.

"I don't see anyone," she whispered, taking Harper's hand to give a reassuring squeeze. "If anything happens, you need to run as fast as you can and hide. Do you understand?"

Terri waited for her to nod before leading her back to the opening. She took a deep breath and started to wiggle through the tight fissure. A light clicked on and shined in her face.

"Well, ain't this a hoot," Mike said with a chuckle. "Must be fate, us meeting like this."

Terri's shoulders slumped, and a tiny whimper slipped out. Harper clutched at her mother's back and pressed her face between Terri's shoulder blades.

"Now where's my boy at?" he asked, moving the light so he could see deeper into the tunnel. When neither woman answered, he dropped the light and aimed his shotgun towards them. "Now don't be rude. I asked a question, and I expect an answer."

"He's dead," Terri mumbled. She reached behind her and jammed the flashlight into her daughter's hands. "He fell ... It was an accident."

"Huh," Mike said with a grimace. "I'd say go get me the body, but time's a wastin', and I don't think I want to be here anymore. So why don't y'all come out, and we can split. I promise to be nothing but a gentleman."

Terri shook her head and shifted her left arm to her daughter's hip. She wanted them to be able to move quickly, but she wasn't sure the girl would understand. She pinched her, stopping when she felt Harper stiffen against her. She hoped the girl understood to head back to the beach.

"God damn it, y'all're tryin' my patience. Get your asses out here," he said, keeping his light directly in her face. "Now."

A shadow loomed from behind the big man, and Terri's breath caught. Her eyes grew wide, and her mouth opened to release the scream building in her chest. The Goatman stood behind Mike and pressed a finger against its muzzle. Its lips peeled back in a smile and exposed jagged, gore-encrusted teeth. It raised its other arm high, and the hatchet it held glinted in the firelight.

"Enough of your bullshit," Mike growled, jabbing towards the gap with the barrel. "I'm done playing. GET. OUT."

Terri pushed her hand into her daughter's side and released the scream, her eyes locked on to the hatchet as it swept down and drove into the side of Mike's neck. Blood sprayed from the wound, splashing across Terri's face. The Goatman jerked the hatchet free, grabbed the man by his hair, and swung again, slicing through his neck. The body spasmed, and the shotgun roared, drowning out her screams.

Terri tumbled to the stone floor, her vision washed in red. Her head rocked back, and she watched her daughter shuffling back down the tunnel. *Run, baby, run.* She hoped Harper heard her, but in the end, she wasn't sure she actually spoke the words.

CHAPTER THIRTY-SEVEN

Billy gritted his teeth. He wasn't sure how much longer he could go on without some help. He pictured Mike, Tristan, and Lenny in his head, buried up to their necks in sand. He could see the looks of terror in their eyes, and he imagined what it would be like to crush each one of those traitors' heads with a cinder block. Each one happened in slow motion, the heavy rectangle smashing into the top and splitting through the skin and then their skulls like an overripe melon. Blood and brains splattered out to land with wet smacks against the hard-packed ground.

He couldn't help but laugh at the thought, which quickly turned to a groan as pain flared in his side. He leaned against the wall and shined his light into the darkness. There was nothing there but more tunnel. *Where are the lights?* He shook his head at the thought, not wanting to admit he was lost. *It shoulda been a straight shot.* He glanced back, shined the light, and found more of the same.

Billy sighed and pressed the back of his hand against his forehead. *Burning up.* He knew there was no other choice than to push forward. Not if he wanted a chance to get his revenge. His mind wandered back to the cinder blocks, and he took another step forward.

★★★

Scott touched the wall and, once again, wondered where the rumble was coming from. He thought about turning to ask if Beth knew what caused it but stopped when he spotted a faint light shining up ahead.

"Do you see that?"

She nodded and pushed past him. "It looks like my patio lights. You know, when you decorate for the holidays?"

He reached out to grab her arm, but she pulled away, and he had no choice but to catch up. "Maybe we should be careful," he hissed, but she ignored him and started to jog.

Scott let out a huff and tightened his grip on the machete. *God damn it.* He left the thought unspoken, mindful yelling at her would get him nowhere. She was just as hardheaded as Amber. A lump formed in his throat. He pushed her face out of his head, well aware now was not the time to focus on that ever-growing grief.

The tunnel began to head towards the right, and after a few steps, they came to a fork.

"Follow the lights ... right?" Beth asked, pointing to the soft glow coming from the left.

She didn't wait for an answer and began to jog in that direction. Scott sighed and followed. He noticed the rumble was growing stronger, and a dull roar began to fill his ears. The tunnel dead-ended into another one, which ran perpendicular to the one they just came from. Lights were hanging from the far wall and offered an almost pleasant illumination.

"You don't think ..." Scott trailed off, unable to bring himself to ask the question.

"Who cares who put them up," Beth answered, offering a half-hearted smile. "I'm just grateful we can see where we're going. So which way now?"

Harper remembered the line running across the tunnel exit right before she got there. She clicked on the flashlight and stepped over it. Tears ran down her cheeks, and though she wanted to look back, she refused to turn her head. She paused at the top of the hill and strained to hear anything over the low hum that filled her ears ever since the shotgun blast.

Nothing. Not even the gentle lapping of the waves below. Harper bit her bottom lip and prayed her hearing returned. She scrambled forward and kept her eyes on the far side of the beach. She thought there were some rocks there, maybe a place to hide. Then she'd wait for her mother to find her, and maybe the nightmare would finally be over.

CHAPTER THIRTY-EIGHT

Billy almost cried when he saw the first string of lights. He leaned against the wall and took a few deep breaths. He had to be close to one of the exits. Simon promised they would light only the important areas. Of course, the way these last few days had gone, Billy didn't want to get ahead of himself. He shifted, and the wounds in his arm and hip screamed in protest. He gritted his teeth and tried to push the sudden flair of pain back down.

"Motherfucker," he gasped, his vision suddenly blurry. He slid down the wall until he sat onto the cold stone. Closing his eyes, he concentrated on the soft rumble he felt vibrating through the stone. His breathing slowed, and he felt himself nodding off.

"These go on forever," a woman said, her voice echoing down the tunnel.

Billy's eye popped open. *No way.* He turned his head and stared down the lighted tunnel. A man stepped into view and glanced both ways. Billy held his breath, unsure if he was deep enough in the shadows to avoid being seen. The woman appeared next to him and pointed down the opposite way.

"Let's keep following the lights," she offered.

Billy shook his head. *How the fuck did the Pope Lick Princess and Ace meet up down here?* He watched them walk away, and as soon as they were out of sight, he struggled to his feet. He reloaded his shotgun and started forward. He'd give them a chance to help, but he kinda hoped they'd refuse.

Harper didn't find any place on the beach to hide, but she did find another tunnel. She shined the light into the darkness and bit her bottom lip. After a moment, she glanced back and stared at the two bodies on the beach. She didn't really want to stay anywhere near them. She looked at the screwdriver in her hand and grimaced. She almost left it jammed into Lenny's neck, but she knew she needed a weapon. Her stomach rolled, and she tried to ignore the memory of her rocking it back and forth until she could slip it free.

"Enough," Harper whispered, needing to hear a voice, even if it was her own.

She scratched a large H on the wall next to the tunnel before entering. She took a few steps, wincing with each step at the dull ache in her ankle. She focused all her attention on the pain, desperate for anything to stop the memories running through her head like a strobe light—flashes of the waterfall attack, Amber's head disappearing, running through the woods, the screwdriver sinking into Lenny's back, his blood running over her hands, then repeating all over again.

After a few more feet, the pain finally washed it all away. *Momma will come soon ... It's going to be all right.* Deep down, she knew it wasn't true, but she repeated it out loud just the same.

✦✦✦

Beth stuck her head into an opening and found another room. She could make out a few duffle bags, but most of the space was in darkness.

"I wonder why they didn't wire any of the rooms?" she asked over her shoulder.

"Maybe they did," Scott replied, looking into another one a few feet further down. "We just haven't found those yet."

"Well, Princess, I figured they could wait for a later date," a voice wheezed from down the tunnel.

Beth's head snapped around, horror growing on her face. Scott stepped past her and raised the machete. "Stop right there."

Billy kept moving towards them, his shoulder sliding across the stone wall. "I don't think so, Ace," he said through clenched teeth. He raised the shotgun up. "Now how about you drop that pigsticker."

Scott glanced at Beth, who nodded. The machete bounced off the floor with a clang and landed a few feet between them. Billy stopped and took a deep breath. "I want nothing more than to pay you two fuckers back in spades, but I'm willing to let bygones be bygones."

"I don't think so," Scott said with a shake of his head.

"You sure about that, Ace? You wanna to be responsible for another woman's death?"

"Fuck you!" Scott spat the words out and sprang forward.

The shotgun roared, and Scott flew back, landing on the ground in a heap. He issued a strangled mewl, his lips quivering as he spit blood up with every breath. Beth pressed her palms against her ears and stared down at him, not sure how Billy would react if she moved. Blood soaked into Scott's shirt and slowly spread out beneath him. He reached up with a trembling arm, and his hand opened and closed.

Billy straightened and stepped over to the man. He pressed the barrel against his forehead. "Best end his suffering," he said and pulled the trigger. The shotgun roared again, and Scott's head exploded, splashing Billy and Beth with bloody bits.

Vomit sprayed from Beth's mouth, splashing down on the stone floor to mix with the gory mess.

"What about you, Princess?" Billy asked, matter of fact.

Beth wiped the back of her hand across her lips and straightened. She stared at Billy for a few seconds before speaking. "Doesn't seem I have much of a choice."

"There's always a choice, but I'm happy to see you make the right one for a change."

"What do you want?"

He slumped back against the wall and took a few heavy breaths. Her gaze darted to the machete sticking out from under Scott's body. She bit her bottom lip, unsure if she could grab it in time.

"I need to be patched up ... sooner than later. Then we get the fuck out of here."

"And that will be it?"

"Scout's honor," he said, flashing a bloody grin.

"Jesus," she murmured before raising her voice. "Fine. There was a room back this way that might have a first-aid kit. Do you need help walking?"

He shook his head and gestured with the shotgun's barrel to move. "Lead the way. I've still got a little fight left."

CHAPTER THIRTY-NINE

Billy watched Beth fade in and out of focus. He was beginning to think he wasn't going to make it out of the caves. *Can't let those motherfuckers win.*

"What?" Beth asked, her head turned just enough for him to hear her.

He hadn't realized he'd spoken. "Where's Simon?" he asked, the question out before he realized it.

"Dead," she said softly. "Amber too. The Goatman got 'em."

"What are you talking about?" Billy stopped, struggling to comprehend her words.

"The Goatman is real," she said, her voice still a whisper. She turned to face him, her eyes wide and her bottom lip trembling. "He killed them all."

Billy stared at her, unsure what to say. A jolt of pain stole his breath, and he slipped down to one knee. He hunched over and struggled to regain his breath. Darkness crept in from the edge, and he wondered if this was it. Beth's cry of rage bounced down the tunnel, and another wave of pain washed over him as she slammed the flashlight down on his head. He dropped the shotgun and slumped forward to the stone floor.

"You bitch," he growled, reaching out to grab her ankle and pull her down before she could strike him again. She cried out in surprise and landed with a grunt. He jerked her closer and crawled over to pin her down. "I only wish I could make you suffer more."

Billy wrapped his thick hands around her throat and squeezed. Beth's eyes bulged out, and she clawed at his hands and wrists. He glared down at her, his lips pulled back in a lopsided grin. He shifted a bit and brought his full weight onto her chest.

Beth's tongue slipped out and dangled from the corner of her mouth. He squeezed harder and began to laugh as the light faded from her eyes. "That's it, you fucking bitch. Die."

Her body shuddered, and once Billy was sure she was dead, he released his grip. Pain pulsed throughout his body, and the tunnel began to spin. The darkness pushed in, and after a few seconds, he could feel his body begin to sway.

"God damn it," he mumbled before everything went black and he slumped forward to land on Beth's body.

★★★

Harper shuffled forward; at some point, she got turned around and couldn't figure out how to get back to the water. The flashlight's beam was growing weaker, and she wondered just how long she'd been lost in the tunnels. Her stomach growled, but she ignored it, well aware she didn't have anything to eat or drink. Up ahead, she could see that the tunnel crossed with another, and she wondered if maybe she'd already been through this way.

Harper stopped at the cross section. She pointed the light to the left, but it began to flicker.

"No, no, no," she pleaded, shaking the flashlight. The flicker slowed a second, but then the light cut off and plunged her into darkness. A sob ripped from her chest, and she slumped to the floor. She wrapped her arms around her knees and began to rock back and forth.

A hand fell on her shoulder, and she jumped; her shriek echoed though the tunnels.

"Why so sad?" she heard her mother ask from the dark.

Harper spun and reached out to grab hold of her mother. Relief washed over her, but after a few seconds, she realized something was terribly wrong. A thick musk filled her nostrils, and coarse hair covered the legs she now hugged.

A fit of giggles came from the darkness above her, and before Harper began to scream again, she swore she heard a child say, "Silly rabbit."

EPILOGUE

Maddie Jenkins lay as still as possible, desperate not to disturb the filth-soaked mattress beneath her. She tried not to think of the semen, piss, and diarrhea the fabric had been soaking up over the last ten days. *Has it been that long?* Her stomach rumbled, pulling her attention back to the hollow ache in her belly. She blinked back the sudden tears, surprised to discover her body still had enough moisture left to produce them. She glanced in the direction of where the preacher left a water bottle behind, unsure how much liquid it still held.

"Save those tears," she mumbled to herself for the umpteenth time.

Tiny feet scuttled off to her left. Maddie bit her bottom lip and prayed whatever else was in the room didn't decide to investigate her again. At first, she thought it was a mouse, but now she imagined something larger. Something quite hungry. She scrunched her eyes closed. *ENOUGH*. The word shattered the image in her mind, and she shifted her attention before it could form again. Tapping her fingertips together, she began to count. The chains that held her arms above her head were taut, causing the metal shackles to cut into her wrists, and she found this was the only way to get the circulation going again. Every time she stopped, it was much harder to start up again.

The creature's footsteps grew closer.

Maddie ignored them, focusing on her fingers and the numbers she knew were failing to distract her from her ever-darkening thoughts. She was so thirsty, but her fingers needed more feeling if she hoped to maneuver the water bottle over to her lips. *What if I fail?* So instead of trying, she continued to count.

The tingling in her palms was a good thing, right? A loud creak sounded above and chased the thought away. For a moment, she wondered if it was real, but as the silence stretched on, she decided it was all in her head. Maddie swung her head back to stare where she thought the bottle was, her bloody, cracked lips aching in anticipation. Taking a deep breath, Maddie willed her hand to move, her fingertips sliding against the plastic.

"Please," she croaked, her body trembling from the effort.

Stretching, she ignored the streaks of pain shooting through her limbs and was rewarded with the crackling of the plastic as her hand gripped the bottle. Agony shot through her shoulders with every movement, but soon she was holding the bottle above her head. Maddie whispered a prayer, begging for the strength to hold it. *No matter how good it will feel on my skin, please don't let me waste a drop.* Maddie tilted the bottle. A stream of water fell through the darkness, striking her mouth and slipping through her lips. A spasm twisted her back, and her hand went numb, releasing the bottle.

"God, no," she whimpered.

The plastic bottle struck her cheek, splashing her with water. She flailed her head, searching for it with her mouth and tongue. It slid onto the mattress, the final drops dribbling out to join the muck below her. Her sob turned into a wordless howl.

"Did you hear that?" a muffled voice said in the darkness.

Maddie ignored it and continued to scream. The voices had been visiting on and off for days, and she knew they were no more real than the creak from before.

"There."

"Yeah … I think you're right," another voice answered.

"Shit, this lock is … got it."

A piece of metal snapped, and a rectangle of light appeared. Maddie's scream cut off. *He's back … back to punish me more.* Her eyes slammed shut as the light grew closer.

"Jesus Christ … what the fuck," the voice said, gagging throughout.

"The smell alone," the other voice replied, suddenly muffled. "A pillar of the community, my ass. What was that dude up to?"

"This poor woman and—God damn it," the voice said, retching off to the side.

Maddie opened her eyes to a slit, struggling to make out the shapes before her. After a moment, her eyes widened, and another tear slipped free as she took in her exposed body. Her skin was red and splotchy, and oozing sores covered her in a dull slime. Her matted pubic hair stuck to her thighs and belly. A thick, black zip tie secured her ankles, leaving her feet a pale white. It occurred to her she could not remember the last time she felt her toes move. A low moan slipped past her lips.

"Ma'am, help is on the way. We've got paramedics in the area," the voice said before asking. "Do you remember anything?"

She shook her head, still unsure if anyone was actually in the room with her. A commotion sounded above, and soon hands began to move around her, gently probing and shifting. *This is real?* Pain and relief flooded her, sending her in and out of consciousness.

"I'm telling you," a woman said, "that sick fuck got exactly what he deserved out in those woods."

"Yeah. I mean, who would have believed a preacher capable of … this," a deep male voice replied.

The woman continued with a forced laugh, "In fact, being hacked to pieces was probably too good for that scumbag. They said parts were missing. We both know what that means."

"Shit. No one believes that stuff. It's just a myth. An urban legend."

"I saw a picture of the hoof prints. Ain't no goat making those tracks and killing all those people *with an axe*."

Suddenly, Maddie was floating, covered in a crinkling blanket that made her feel warm and toasty. Her eyes fluttered open. The light blinded her for a moment, but it cleared after a few blinks. A shadowy face looked down at her, and for a moment, she thought she saw horns.

"Don't worry, honey, you're safe now."

Her eyes closed, and as she drifted off, she heard the woman continue:

"I'm telling you, the Goatman is real and the only reason this poor thing is alive."

THE END

THE POPE LICK MASSACRE

There are two types of people in Jefferson County: those who know the legend of the Pope Lick Monster and those who believe it. Before the night is over, Sam will have no choice but to join the believers.

Since their mother's death, Sam's sole focus has been taking care of her younger brother, Kenny. Now Kenny's Scout troop is missing, having never returned from the woods around Pope Lick. Sam gathers a group of friends to search for the boys and their Scoutmaster. With each step, they get closer to discovering the scouts aren't the only ones in the woods this night.

"The Pope Lick Massacre is a bold, brutal horror story that'll remain in your mind long after you read it. This book is not for the faint of heart." –Independent Book Review

"Eric Butler crossed a bold line in this book, and I loved it." – **Sea Caummisar**, author of the *Raised By A Killer* series.

Centuries ago, the native people imprisoned a spirit of pure evil and unending hunger. Thirteen years ago, an eight-year-old boy woke the darkness. It grows in strength every day, and now that the boy is a man, adept in terror and violence, the darkness hopes to finally break free.

And here Jill thought the scariest thing on this vacation was going to be spending the week with her boyfriend's kids.

The Independent Book Review says, "Author Eric Butler turns a long-awaited trip home into a lustful, gruesome, and horrific summer. Be ready for it. This novel might just make you double-lock your doors tonight."

THE SHADOW WITHIN

The Ephraim Godwin Chronicles

The Sins of the Past

Once an ancient race of supreme beings ruled over the earth. Banished by the light centuries ago, one has returned. With the help of its disciples, it desires to plunge the world into a new age of darkness and horror.

Ephraim Godwin is searching for the truth about his family's disappearance. After conventional ways failed, he turned to the world of spiritualism, only to discover it filled with charlatans and tricksters. As a known skeptic, Ephraim fights to shine a light on those who prey upon others as he searches for the truth.

As Ephraim attends another séance, he discovers not everyone is a fraud and is drawn deeper into the world of the supernatural. With the help of noted spiritualist Zona Whitlock and famed explorer Doctor Livingstone, he hopes to stop this evil from consuming the world.

THE DONN, TX COLLECTION VOLUME 1 IN PAPERBACK

There's a place in Texas the locals avoid, where the lost go missing and the damned reside. You won't find it on any map, there are no road signs to guide you, and if you have the misfortune of finding it, may God have mercy on your soul.
Run, run as far as you can, for when The Scarecrow wakes, the harvest of blood begins.

Welcome to Donn, TX - Gateway to Hell.

COLLECTS THE EBOOKS

DONN, TX 1952

DONN, TX 1969

DONN, TX 1865

DONN, TX 1926

DONN, TX 2002

Patrick Smite is now following in his father's footsteps as the sheriff of Donn, TX. His sister, Laura, is worried he won't be able to do all the job requires. For while he believes he can keep the town safe, she knows the awful truth: they must honor the family's obligation to The Pale Man, no matter the cost.

Danielle Kipler is on the run. The Pale Man in her dreams promised her sanctuary. The only thing required is her undying allegiance. But is she prepared to make the necessary sacrifices to become a citizen of Donn, TX?

Years ago, a pact was made that requires payment in blood. For in the end, all that matters is the harvest.

FIND IT ON EBOOK, PAPERBACK, &

AUDIOBOOK

DONN, TX 1978

Sheriff Harold Smite has done all he can to make the yearly harvest run smoothly, but something out in the corn is dying to get free.

Jane Lipman faced the harvest nine years ago and survived. She's done everything she can to make peace with the past, but Donn, TX isn't done with her.

Bonnie Smite thought she was simply run down, but she's been chosen for something special. Something only The Pale Man knows about and he's not sharing.

Welcome to Donn, TX: Gateway to Hell.

There's Something In The Water

Expanded Edition

All Kurt Reedy needed for his lakeside development project to go through was the land owned by Chuck Miller. The only problem was Miller refused to sell his family's legacy. In the past, Reedy may have resorted to violence to get his way, but he was a legit businessman now.

Running out of time, he is forced to think outside the box. In his haste, he doesn't do the proper research, and now there's something in the water.

Something territorial.

Something hungry.

THE SURROGATE

In their search for a surrogate, the Wilkenses thought they struck gold with Alina. All she wanted was a flight to the United States and a warm place to stay during the pregnancy.

But some things are too good to be true ...

Kiss Me Where It Smells Funny

Alex has a crush on the new Teacher's assistant, and he's finally worked up the nerve to approach her.

Too bad she's crossed the University's star player, and Duncan Shaw has no choice but to make her disappear.

He plans to lay the blame on the local urban legend, but tonight he just might learn that some legends are real.

TO STARE DEATH IN THE EYES EXTREME EDITION

There's something preying on the locals, and Irving Fontaine has no choice but to investigate. He heads toward the unknown armed with his wits, a Colt 1860, and a warning from a mysterious Indian.

Avoid the hills that stare with dead eyes, for there, the soulless wait to bring despair when the shadows awake to feed again.

Read the author's preferred extreme horror edition of To Stare Death in The Eyes and discover monsters are everywhere.

THE
REST STOP

The author of *The Popelick Massacre* and *Donn, TX* returns with a grindhouse tale in the vein of *TCM* and *House of 1000 Corpses*.

A rest stop with a reputation for abandoned cars in the middle of nowhere and a family on their way to a new home turns into a tale of terror.

Sometimes it's better to keep driving, no matter how tired you are.

ABOUT THE AUTHOR

I'm an indie Horror writer who lives deep in the heart of Texas. When I'm not writing novels and stories for anthologies, I'm doing the bidding of two adorable huskies. I've been married for over twenty years and have a teenager in the house, so I won't be running out of horror material for quite some time. Enter a world of horror ...

Thanks for reading! Please add a short review on Amazon and let me know what you thought!

Don't forget to sign up at www.EricButlerAuthor.com for exciting news on upcoming projects.

READ INDIE HORROR
AND FEED A HUSKY